# Mystery Lights
# *of* Navajo Mesa

# Mystery Lights of Navajo Mesa



**Jake Thoene and Luke Thoene**

Based on the story and characters
created by Robert Vernon
and the screenplay by Jake Thoene, Luke Thoene,
Brock Thoene, and Bodie Thoene.

Tyndale House Publishers, Inc.
WHEATON, ILLINOIS

Published in association with the literary agency of Alive Communications,
P.O. Box 49068, Colorado Springs, CO 80949



---

**Library of Congress Cataloging-in-Publication Data**

Thoene, Jake.
Mystery lights of Navajo Mesa / Jake Thoene and Luke Thoene.
p. cm. — (Focus on the Family presents The last chance detectives ; 1)
Based on the story and characters created by Robert Vernon and the screenplay by Jake Thoene, Luke Thoene, Brock Thoene, and Bodie Thoene.
Summary: While investigating the robbery of a local museum, four young friends see some mysterious lights that they believe belong to a UFO on the mesa near the fictional town of Ambrosia, Arizona, and find themselves in real danger.
ISBN 0-8423-2082-2
[1. Mystery and detective stories. 2. Arizona—Fiction.]
I. Thoene, Luke. II. Focus on the Family (Organization)
III. Title. IV. Series: Last chance detectives ; 1.
PZ7.T35655My 1994 94-30426
[Fic]—dc20

---

Printed in the United States of America

01 00 99 98 97 96 95
8 7 6 5 4 3

# 1

Twelve-year-old Mike Fowler sat in the pilot's seat of the old B-17 bomber and heard the rattle of machine-gun fire as bullets zipped by the cockpit. Turning sharply to peer over his shoulder down the interior of the plane, Mike watched as his best friend, Ben Jones, maneuvered his weapon in the waist-gunner position.

A voice that sounded like movie star John

Wayne's warned, *"Eighteen Mitzi attack bombers three points to your right—about 15,000 altitude!"*

Mike saw Ben swing the twin machine guns to intercept incoming fighters. He heard a loud banging on the fuselage.

"Mike! We're hit!" Ben yelped. "They blew our left wing off!"

Mike concentrated on controlling the bucking B-17. He shouted at Ben, "No, they didn't blow our wing off! The plane can't fly if the wing is OFF! If they blew our wing off, we're going to die five minutes into the movie and that's it!"

Ben paused to think it over. "Oh . . . oh yeah."

Mike reached behind him and turned up the volume on the combination TV/VCR that was playing the John Wayne movie *The Flying Tigers.*

"Don't try to win this war yourself," Wayne said. *"Stick close to element formation. . . . DING HOW!"*

"Ding how!" Mike shouted.



Ben responded with the same phrase, and both boys returned to their mock battle, the movie providing the sound effects. The banging continued on the outside of the plane. Then Mike heard the voice of his Navajo friend Wynona Whitefeather.

"Hey! Let me in!" she shouted. "Come on, you guys! Mike Fowler! Ben Jones! You open up or I'll . . ."

Mike and Ben chose to ignore her until the

battle was over, then both turned to watch the screen as John Wayne exited his plane.

*"Lookie, Cap'n Jim!"* a Chinese man shouted, pointing to the bullet holes in Wayne's fighter. *"Lookie! Wham! Wham!"*

Winnie was still yelling as John Wayne's deep voice remarked to the man, *"Termites."*

"Come on, guys! Let me in!"

Mike and Ben looked at each other and shouted in unison, "Wynona!" Ben ran down the length of the fuselage to let her in.

"Why didn't you let me in?!" she yelled at Ben. "I've been knocking out there forever!"

"Gee, Winnie," Ben said innocently, "I guess we didn't hear you."

"Don't gimme that, you overgrown sack of pork rinds!"

Ben stepped back and looked to his pilot friend for help. "Honest. Huh, Mike? We thought you were enemy flack or somethin', didn't we, Mike?"

"Nope," Mike said, and Ben sank into a chair when his alibi disappeared. "But you were late, Winnie, so we started without you."

Winnie accepted Mike's explanation with a shrug.

"You didn't think we'd open the hatch at fifteen thousand feet, did you?" Ben asked.

"Mind your own business, Ben. I have my own reason for being late."

"Better be good," Ben said quietly.

Winnie stomped her foot down. Ben thought she was going to hit him, and he jumped, almost knocking over the chair. The Navajo girl turned and shouted through the entry, "OK, Spencer. Come on up!"

"Hold it," Ben said as an unknown boy climbed in through the hatch. "No unauthorized personnel . . ."

Winnie ignored Ben and explained to Mike, "His name is Spencer Martin. A real brain. His dad's some kind of scientist. He hired my dad to guide him to the old cliff dwellings at the lake. Dad says if we show Spence around, we can use the quad runners while they're gone. Spencer," she said when the newcomer joined the group, "this is Mike Fowler, our captain. . . ."

"And I'm Ben Jones," Ben said self-importantly. "I'm the waist gunner."



Mike noticed that, while Spencer was not impressed with Ben, he loved the plane.

"Wow! A Flying Fortress," Spencer said. "B-17. I've seen pictures. E-type isn't it? Sperry ball turret. Perfect condition. Really amazing in a place like this." Spencer paused to clean his glasses on the tail of his plaid shirt, replacing them over alert brown eyes that were the same color as his skin.

"We use it as headquarters for our detective agency. We call ourselves the Last Chance Detectives," Winnie said. "It belongs to Pop Fowler, Mike's grandfather."

"Pop flew her in the war," Mike said proudly. "Rescued her from a junkyard down in Kingman and restored pretty much everything himself."

"I'll say," Spencer said, very impressed. "Wright Cyclone engines. Cruising speed two hundred seventy-six miles an hour. Top speed—"

Ben interrupted, "Pop Fowler was a famous pilot . . . and Mike's dad was in the news too. He was the air force pilot . . . I mean *is* the pilot in Operation Desert Storm who . . ."

Winnie glared at him, and Ben stopped talking, leaving an awkward silence. Spencer blinked through his glasses, wondering if anyone would explain.

"Any good cases today?" Mike asked, changing the subject.

Winnie, very businesslike, opened her leather-bound notebook.

Mike leaned forward to look at the list. Meanwhile, Spencer and Ben walked through the plane and looked at the controls. Spencer stopped at the radio. "Terrific!" he said. "All original equipment. Mind if I try it out?"

Mike took his place in the cockpit just in time

to see the sheriff's patrol truck pull up on the airfield. It stopped next to the twin-engined Beechcraft, which Mike's grandfather had just finished fueling.

Sheriff Arnold Smith had lived in Ambrosia all his life. Everyone in the town knew him, and most everyone called him Sheriff Smitty, or just Smitty. Smitty was a big man, middle-aged and graying. Though he had no children, he thought of the Last Chance Detectives as his own and was very close to the Fowler family. This closeness explained why he felt he could ask Pop Fowler for a big favor.

Smitty shut off the engine of his brown-gold Chevy. He straightened his uniform, brushing off some flecks of dark red dust, and headed for the door of the hangar.

Pop Fowler met him halfway. "How are you, Smitty?" Pop asked with a smile in his voice. Mike could hear Pop's voice drifting up through the open window of the B-17.



"Oh, I'm doin' OK," Smitty replied, chewing his gum.

Long before, Pop and others had figured out that Smitty always chewed gum when he was thinking and the harder he chewed, the deeper were the thoughts. Right now the sheriff's jaw was working rapidly. "Well, come on over to the diner," Pop invited, "and I'll get you something."

Smitty declined the suggestion. "I'm sorry, Pop. Strictly business today. Come to ask you a favor."

"Anything . . . except loan you money." Pop chuckled at his own humor. The lines on Pop's wrinkled forehead crinkled beneath his white hair.

"Naw, nothing like that. I need you to run me up in the *Liberty.* I've come into some business that I can't take care of on the ground."

"That's no problem," Pop said eagerly. "You know I'm always lookin' for an excuse to fly 'er."

"All right then," Smitty said, "I'd like to get crackin' ASAP, but I can't explain more now—sorry."

Mike heard Pop call him.

"Hey, guys," Pop said as he appeared, standing in the hatch from the waist up, "I've got to take Smitty up in the plane, but we'll be back in about an hour. You can have the clubhouse back then."

"Aw, Pop, can't we go?" Mike asked.

"Hold on," Pop said. "I'll ask Smitty."

Mike listened intently as Smitty gave his answer from the outside.

"No problem," Smitty said. "Be glad to have them along."

"You heard him," Pop said with a smile. "So buckle up and get ready."

The gang cheered when they heard, and Smitty climbed aboard. Spencer's eyes grew wide with amazement. Mike guessed that their new friend had not really expected to go aloft in the vintage aircraft.

"All right, guys," Pop cautioned, "remember this is a business trip, so keep the noise down."

Smitty took his seat and clicked his gum as Pop started the engines. A cloud of pale blue smoke belched from one after another of the four exhausts as the B-17 roared to life. "Now about this business trip," Smitty explained as they taxied onto the runway. Pop handed him a pair of earphones with a microphone attached.

"These'll make it easier to talk over the engine noise," Pop yelled.

Mike listened with interest on his own headset as Smitty slipped on the equipment and began talking. "I can't give you details, but I've been asked to keep an eye on anything suspicious in my area. Ambrosia's too small to keep something secret for very long, and outside of town there's so much desert, the only way to keep an eye on it is from the air."



Pop nodded, happy to help out.

The surge of excitement Mike felt when he heard about the supicious activity mixed with the drop of his stomach as the *Lady Liberty* pulled off the runway and lifted into the air. Pop began turning when he was at five hundred feet, and the plane swung back over Ambrosia.

Mike could see everything. Along the main street was the Last Chance Diner on one side, the hangar on the other. Farther up was one of the two little motels in town, with the tepee-shaped Navajo souvenir shop right next to it. Dirt roads peeled off from the highway and led to houses scattered throughout and behind the town.

They were gaining altitude, and it was getting harder to see details on the ground. In the distance, just north of the town, he could see his house, located close to Smitty's and the sheriff's office.

"So where to, Smitty?" Pop asked.

"Well, how about the northwest mesa area to start? Then we can work our way south from there."

"Roger," Pop replied, and they banked left. Mike's stomach jumped again.

"Better than a Disneyland ride, eh, Smitty?" Pop asked.

"Wouldn't know," Smitty said. "I've never been to Disneyland."

Pop swung low again once the plane was clear of the town, and they sped over the hot desert on the way to the northwest mesas. Mike had never been there himself, but he had heard they were amazing. And now possibly even mysterious!

Leaning forward to look out of the window, Mike saw the mesas looming in the distance ahead grow larger every second. The mesas were large orange-red mountains that loomed up out of the desert. Their level summits looked as though the tall peaks had gotten flattop haircuts.

"OK," Pop said, slowing the plane with the flaps, "I assume that you want to look them over a little slower than this baby's top speed, huh?" Mike noticed a smile on Pop's face when he said this to Smitty.

"Sure are proud of her, aren't you, Pop?" Mike asked over his headset.

"Just a little," Pop replied, setting the bomber into a gentle circle around the tabletop mountains. Soon they swung south as Smitty scanned the ground for anything unusual. The sun was already sinking, and soon it would be too dark to see.

"We're not quite going to get to the southwest quadrant today before our light runs out," Pop said.

"That's all right," Smitty agreed. "We'll finish up here and maybe get to the southwest next week. Doesn't look like there's anything going on anyway."

Mike studied the desert floor too. *There is a mystery here yet,* he thought. *And I'm going to find it someday.*

# 2

A week after Spence joined the group, the plane's radio was still not fixed. No exciting cases had come up, but the B-17 continued its duty as the perfect clubhouse for the Last Chance Detectives. Wanted posters and news clippings about crimes were plastered on the walls. Stacks of comic books were within easy reach of Ben as he munched chips and glanced through his latest magazine while Winnie checked her list of cases.

Mike entered through the hatch and looked around at the mess.

"Mike!" Ben greeted him over a mouthful of chips.

"Hey, Ben, what's up?"

Ben washed down chips with a gulp of Coke, then held up a comic book in a plastic bag. "Check it out!" Ben said proudly. "Silver Surfer #1. Premier issue!"

"Cool!" Mike replied with admiration for the prize.

Ben gushed on happily about the story. "This is the one where he gets exiled to planet Earth after—"

Winnie broke in, "I hate to interrupt this deep discussion about comic books, but don't we have a meeting to begin?"



Ben gawked at her. "Winnie, this is not just a comic book! This is John Buscoma at the top of his art form. This is a Stan Lee at his literary peak! It's a milestone. It—"

"It'll turn your brain to mush!" Winnie remarked with disdain.

"Oh yeah?" Ben protested. "Well, for your information this is gonna be worth a lot of money someday."

"See what I mean?" Winnie said to Mike.

For a moment, it seemed as if an argument might break out between Winnie and Ben. Luckily, Spence arrived just in time to distract the two.

Carrying a paper bag, Spence called, "Hi! Sorry I'm late."

"Hi," Mike greeted him.

"Watch out for Winnie," Ben said. "She's in a bad mood."

Spence pulled an old radio tube triumphantly out of the bag. "Well, this oughta cheer things up. Look what finally arrived!"

Ben burped loudly. "What's that?"

Spence explained with pride, "It's a super heterodyne tube! For the radio! Remember? I've been trying to fix it!" His three friends still did not understand the importance of the tube. Spence shrugged and went back to work on the radio.

Mike, Ben, and Winnie discussed possible investigations as Spencer resumed his interrupted examination of the radio.

"Anything goin' besides lost cats?" Mike asked.

Winnie shook her head sadly, tossing her long, dark brown hair. "Miss Tug lost another cat last night."

"Some coyote's gettin' real fat. No."

Winnie nodded and checked off the cat. Then she brightened. "Mister Drummond's offering a five-dollar reward if anyone finds his mother's false teeth."

"Wait! I've got those!" Ben reached into a bag and held up a set of gag false teeth. He wound them and set them chattering on the table.

Mike sighed, "Don't we have anything good for a change? These cases aren't exactly worthy of Sherlock Holmes, but hey, we've got to start somewhere."

It seemed hopeless to Mike. Wouldn't they ever get a really good case? The detective team had plenty going for it.

The newcomer, Spence, was a real brain. He had quickly taken his place as computer expert. It was hard to think of something that he was not an expert in.

Then there was Winnie Whitefeather. Of course, she had a temper like Donald Duck, but there were a lot of great qualities to make up for it. A full-blooded Navajo, her grandmother ran the trading post in town. She provided the pipeline for the latest news. If ever there was a question about Ambrosia, Winnie could find the answer. She knew the desert like the back of her hand.

And Ben? He did a lot of the legwork and

generally filled in the cracks. Assuming that Mike could pull him away from his TV set. Mike thought that Ben had more imagination than the rest of the agency put together. Ben was the kind of guy who thought every housefly was a killer bee in disguise. He kept life interesting.

As for Mike, he was the leader of the Last Chance Detectives. It was his job to hold the group together and find interesting cases to solve. It was not always easy, but sometimes the best mysteries popped up where they were least expected.

"I wonder what that was all about with Sheriff Smitty last week?" Winnie asked. "It must be something big if he couldn't talk about it. Maybe he'd let us—"

"Fat chance, Wynona," Ben scoffed. "Think Smitty is gonna let us have a look at his files?"

Winnie chose to ignore Ben's mocking. "It wouldn't hurt for us to poke around in the desert, would it Mike? After all, Sheriff Smitty's looking out there—maybe something really big's goin' on."

Mike shrugged. "I wish there was a connection and we could find it. Maybe then people would take our detective agency seriously. But Sheriff Smitty said it: There's a whole lot of desert out there. How would we know where to start? We don't even know what it was all about."

Spence, settled into the radio operator's chair, began flipping switches and turning knobs. Spencer was a bit uncomfortable at being new and not really feeling a part of the group. He wished there were some way he could prove his value to the Last Chance Detectives. Maybe then he'd be more than just "the new kid."

"It doesn't work," Ben warned again about the fifty-year-old equipment. At that instant, Spencer flipped a toggle switch and the radio speaker hissed. "Bingo!" Spence said. A gentle humming came from the insides of the unit as the tubes warmed up, and Ben moved in closer, obviously impressed.

"So, how do you know so much about B-17s?" Ben continued.

"A hobby," Spencer said modestly. "We lived near the aerospace museum in D.C. when I was small." He continued fiddling with the knobs. All that could be heard from the speaker were hissing and roaring noises.



Trying to sound like an authority, Ben said, "Pop might not like you messing with that. I told you it doesn't wor—"

Whining loudly in a high screech that swooped down in pitch, the radio came suddenly to life. A wicked sounding voice was heard, crystal clear in tone but spouting nonsense words. Mike and

Winnie jumped up from their seats and forgot all about the list of Ambrosia mysteries.

*"Ae . . . Nav . . . quest . . . Nez,"* the voice from the radio grumbled.

"Doesn't work, huh, Ben?" Winnie asked triumphantly.

"Well," Mike said in defense of Ben, "it never did before now."

"Yeah!" Ben agreed.

Spence looked at the radio in amazement. "But there shouldn't . . . this frequency hasn't been used since—"

*"San . . . Nati . . . Fee . . . Natani Nez,"* the rasping voice continued.

"Is that Spanish?" Ben asked.

"It's like no language I've ever heard," Spencer answered, touching a fine-tuning knob on the set.

The voice continued speaking but was gradually fading.

*"Ekas . . . ekul . . . etor sidkoob,"* it said fiercely, sending a shudder of fear up the spines of the four detectives. What meaning was hidden in the terrible-sounding voice? Then it repeated the secret code once again and vanished.

"Weird," Winnie said. "I mean . . . really weird. It sounded like it said Natani Nez at first and then . . . I don't know."

Ben allowed his imagination to go wild. "I

heard this kind of language in *Invasion from Mars,* where the aliens take over everyone's brain."

"No danger to you then," Winnie said.

"Oh yeah?" Ben retorted. "They prob'ly wouldn't want—"

Interrupting the teasing match before it got rolling, Spencer commented, "Sorry to disappoint you, but a radio like this can only pick up transmissions broadcast from a few miles away at most. Outer space is definitely out. VLF: Very Low Frequency. It's just garbled, or in some kind of code."

"We need a good radioman in this crew, Spence," Mike said to Spence. "Glad you wanted to enlist. Is there any way we can find where this is coming from?"

"Well, maybe," Spence replied. "It would take me a few hours, but if I could modify this Omega receiver, we could lock on to the transmission and pinpoint its origin."



"Great," Mike said with excitement in his voice. Go for it." Then to Winnie, *"Natani?* What does that mean?"

"It's the Navajo word for leader. *Natani Nez* means 'tall leader.' Could be a person or the rock formation on the mesa."

"Navajo Mesa?" Mike asked. "We oughta check that out."

"Now, hold on!" Ben protested. "What if it's like an alien life form or something?"

"Come on, Ben," Winnie mocked. "Don't tell me that now we've finally found a real mystery, you're turning chicken on us!"

"Chicken!" Ben sputtered. "Winnie, I'm no chicken."

"Look," Mike interrupted. "We'll put it to a vote. All those in favor of investigating the mesa say aye."

Everyone voted in favor of the investigation, and the Last Chance Detectives were on the case.

# 3

Mike grabbed his compass from the cockpit visor and dashed down the length of the B-17's cabin. He plunged out of the hatch like a veteran airman and never missed a step. Winnie was right behind, and Spencer followed her. Moments later Ben clambered down, stumbled backwards, and nearly fell, yelling, "Hey, guys! Wait for me—wait for me!"

Jumping onto the blue quad runner that had a lunch basket strapped to the equipment rack, Mike started up the engine with a loud roar. He raised his arm in the Last Chance salute and saw Winnie return it as she pulled on her helmet. Spencer was calmly inspecting the quad as Ben scrambled from beneath the airplane to mount his.

When everyone had helmets on and quads fired up, Mike turned and peeled out. His machine kicked up two rooster tails of dust as he jetted off toward the mesa.

Out in front of the group stood the mesas, looking like the stumps of huge trees way off in the desert. The sun was beating down, and Mike enjoyed the breeze caused by the motion of the quad.

Knowing the general direction he wanted to go, Mike remembered a cactus-filled ravine that headed the same way. It was a creek bed in the rare times of flash floods that coursed down from the mesas. Now its rim was the perfect highway to lead them into their investigation.



Mike saw Winnie pull up on his left side, then Spencer joined them on the right. The three leaders were now in a kind of arrow shape. Ben was behind the others, getting a faceful of their dust. Mike turned toward Winnie and gave a left-handed salute to his helmet, then gassed his quad and pulled far into the lead. The race was on!

Ben spotted a gap between Mike and Winnie and, jetting ahead, cut her off, causing her to swerve and dive down into the ravine, where Mike lost sight of her. Spencer, being lighter than Mike, was steadily pulling up on him and soon passed him. Mike swerved to his right to try and loop around on the outside, but Spencer also moved to the right and kept him in second. This jockeying for position continued, reminding Mike of an Indianapolis 500 race he had seen where the first-place car kept swerving to keep his opponent from getting by.

Mike was wondering where Winnie had gone when suddenly, just ahead of the three boys, she jumped her quad out of the canyon right in front of them. Her abrupt reappearance caused Spencer to slam on the brakes, and Mike nearly ran into him.



The front of Winnie's quad was covered in green hunks of plants, and when Mike looked back into the arroyo from which she had emerged, he saw a trail of fallen cactus as if a huge lawn mower had gone through.

Ben swerved around the confusion and got into second place behind Winnie. Mike was brought out of his daydreaming as Spencer took off again, pumping smelly exhaust fumes into his face. Mike hurriedly accelerated, racing toward the front of the pack.

Ahead, Winnie was still in first place, but Spencer had already passed Ben and was catching up to her. Winnie tried to swerve to keep him behind, but he faked a move to the left and then quickly turned to the right and passed her.

Mike saw that Ben was moving way out on the other side then noticed that the ravine made a sweeping right turn just ahead of them. When Mike spotted it, he peeled off to the right and quickly overtook Ben, congratulating himself for being in first place after the shortcut. He slowed a little and looked back at Winnie and Spence still battling it out as they rounded the curve of the streambed that Mike and Ben had just plunged across.

A short distance ahead, the ravine swung left again and climbed into the foothills at the base of the mesas. Mike figured that this would be a good place to check their map, so he slowed to a stop on top of a red mound of earth and got off. Ben drove by him at full speed, as if he thought that the race was still on and Mike was having trouble with his engine. Winnie and Spence got the right idea and skidded to a halt close to Mike. Fifty yards ahead, Ben looked back, realized his mistake, and turned around.

"Well," Mike said, "are you guys hungry?"

"Gettin' there," said Winnie.

"I could use a little nourishment," Spence added.

"OK, then, we know Ben'll be hungry, so how about we head to that high spot and break out the lunch." He pointed to a knob of rock across the ravine that rose above the desert.

Just then Ben pulled up and took off his helmet. "Hey, guys," he said. "I'm hungry! When do we eat?"

"Never!" Winnie said. "We're gonna keep going all day!"

"Aw, no! Hey, I'm a growing boy! I need to eat," Ben whined. Then a relieved look crossed Ben's face as he remembered something. Reaching into his jacket pocket, he removed a half-eaten, partly melted Three Musketeers candy bar.



"We're just giving you a hard time, Ben," Mike said. "We're going up on that knob to survey the mesa and to have lunch."

The other three kids fired up their quads and rode off toward the red-and-orange outcropping of boulders. Ben started to replace the candy bar, then stopped and studied it. The wrapper had streaked his hands with melted chocolate. The spray of fine dust from his friends' machines coated his fingers and the candy. Ben looked at the dirt, shrugged his shoulders, and ate the candy anyway, licking the dusty chocolate off his fingers. Then he set off after the others.

On top of the rock formation, Mike unpacked the basket that was strapped to his quad. He passed out the ham and cheese sandwiches, Cokes, chips, and apples that his grandmother had packed for them.

When everyone had their food, Mike began talking about the race on the way out, and everyone joined in.

"You blasted out of that ravine, Winnie," Mike said. "It was amazing!"

"It was nothing," she said with a pleased smile.

"Nufin'," Ben said with his mouth full of ham sandwich. "Fe come fwyin owda wavine—," he swallowed, then finished his sentence—"like a rocket and calls it nothing. Ha!"



It really was quite amazing," Spencer said. "I enjoyed racing on the quad runners!"

Replaying the race occupied the four friends for a time, then Winnie and Mike moved to the edge of the ridge to compare the landscape to their map.

Passing his compass to Winnie, Mike unfolded the chart. "Winnie, can you help me with this?" he asked.

"Sure, but I think I already know where we are."

Mike pointed at the cover of the heavy brass instrument that his father had given him. "Open it and hold it against the map."

Meanwhile, Ben and Spence were talking a few yards back.

Spence looked at Mike thoughtfully. "A natural leader, isn't he?"

"Mike? Yeah, he's a real great guy . . . regular salt of the dirt, ya know?"

"I believe you mean salt of the earth?"

"Whatever . . . a great guy."

"What was that . . . back at the airplane last week . . . about his father?"

"His dad disappeared over Iraq. He's been missing in action for a couple years, and some people think he's not coming back."

"But Mike still believes he's alive?"

"Sure. I've been around him long enough that I believe it too. Me and Winnie both do. Mike's mom and grandparents believe it too, but everyone else has given up." In a thoughtful voice Ben added, "One of these days we're gonna take that old B-17 and fly her to Iraq. We'll find Mike's dad, all right."

Mike sat staring out across the desert. He was holding the small pocket Bible that his father had given him along with the compass.

Winnie looked at him and then at the Bible in his hands. She followed Mike's gaze across the red rock mesa. "Is something wrong, Mike? You sure got quiet."

"Yeah? Well, I was just thinking about my dad."

An afternoon wind picked up on the mesa, and Mike closed his eyes. He could clearly remember the day his father gave the things to him with the advice: *Always keep these close to you, and you'll never be lost.*

Winnie put her hand on Mike's arm. "I pray for him all the time, Mike."

With a shrug and a sad smile Mike replied, "Thanks, Winnie. I just wish my dad had these instead of me."

Back with Spence and Ben, the mood was entirely different. Ben was just getting wound up. "Did you notice anything strange about Winnie's brothers and sisters?"

Spence thought it over. "No, but there sure are a lot of them."



Ben said triumphantly, "Eight! And their names all sound like country-western stars—Reba, Clint, Travis. . . . She hates it when I call her brother Kenny, the Gambler. But if you really want to get to her, just call her house the Grand Ol' Opry!"

"She seems really . . . nice," Spence said, kicking over a rock. A small, dark green scorpion scurried for cover under another stone.

Ben studied the creature intently. "But you haven't seen her *really* mad." He poked at the scorpion with a stick, and a sly smile came over his face. "Watch this."

Sneaking up behind Winnie, Ben motioned for Spence to follow him. He stopped a half dozen feet away and lightly tossed the twig onto Winnie's back. "Look out! Scorpion!"

Winnie jumped up off her rock, clawing at her shoulder. The compass gleamed as it flew through the air, crashing heavily, face first, into a jagged lump of rock.

The noise of the exploding crystal sounded like a gunshot in the still desert air. Winnie's scream was cut off as all four kids realized what had just happened. A horrified silence hung over them.

"Oh, Mike," Winnie pleaded, "I'm sorry!"

Retrieving the smashed compass, Mike walked away from the group and stood facing the empty desert.



Winnie turned her fury on Ben, who backed up abruptly from the anger on the girl's face. "You! You made me break Mike's compass! You weirdo!"

"*Me* weird? It was only a stick . . . a joke, right? Besides, you were the one holding it, not me,

*Miss Wynona Whitefeather!"* Ben's voice took on a mocking, western twang.

"You don't know when to quit, do you, Ben? Don't know when to keep your big mouth shut!"

Ben spoke to Mike, anxious to get the incident over with. "It's just a compass, right, Mike? I'll buy you another one."

Mike whirled around and shouted, "It's not just a compass! It was the compass my dad gave me!"

"But it was just an accident! I'm really sorry!"

Winnie was yelling too. "It's always just something with you, Ben! I'm sick of it!"

Mike clenched his fists in anger and frustration.

Ben's face fell. "It wasn't my idea to come out here in the first place," he pleaded.

In a low, cold tone Mike said, "Nobody's asking you to stay."

"Well, fine!" Ben's voice showed his hurt. "I'm outta here!"

Mike, Spence, and Winnie watched as Ben stormed back to his quad runner and sped off, leaving behind a cloud of dust.



Spence tried to lighten the mood. "Are we still going to investigate the mystery signal?"

Mike was already tromping heavily toward his quad. He shook his head glumly. "Naw . . . I don't feel like it now. . . . Tomorrow. Let's head back."

The grinding hum of the quad runner kept a constant pace with Ben's thoughts as he headed south into the desert. His course took him over boulder-strewn hills and through cactus-choked gulleys.

Ben's anger and frustration stayed with him as he traveled farther into the barren landscape. The bleak canyons and the sharp edges of the unfriendly rocks mirrored the way he felt. What did Winnie know anyway? How could Mike take her side? Ben knew that the breaking of the compass had been his fault, but he was still hurt that his best friend was so cold. Did Mike not know that it had been an accident, a joke? Ben never meant to cause any harm.

The sun sank lower, greeting the red tips of the mesas as it did every afternoon, but Ben paid no attention. He was so turned inward, dwelling on his thoughts, that he did not notice how far or in what direction he was going.



The wind cooled Ben's sweaty arms, and he shivered. A dust devil swirled across a plain of tumbleweeds, throwing a cone of dirt into the early evening sky. Ben's attention was diverted to the miniature tornado, and he leaned into a turn on the quad to chase the airborne spiral. Revving the gas, he jumped a bank of dark red earth and tore through the bushes instead of going around them.

Distracted by his game, Ben did not notice that a small boulder was hidden in the lengthening shadow of a large clump of sage. The left front tire of the quad smashed into the rock, tossing the vehicle onto two wheels.

Ben's weight was thrown off the quad seat, almost breaking his grip on the handlebars. He fought to force the machine back down on all four tires, barely avoiding a ditch on his right. Frightened, Ben brought the quad to a halt and shut off the engine. He shuddered to think what might have happened if he had wrecked out here all alone.

Not only was Ben by himself but he was confused about his location. He stood on the footboards and scanned his surroundings. The territory was completely unknown. There was not even a familiar peak in the distance that he recognized.



The high-pitched rasping noise of the desert insects surrounded him, and the whine of the breeze through the sandstone canyons swelled. Breaking into a sudden sweat, Ben realized that he was closer to being completely lost than *Z* is to the end of the alphabet.

Ben was successful in retracing the tire marks

left by his quad, but only as far as the first fork of the dry creek bed. There the stone floor of the gulch showed no trace of his trail, and a trio of all too similar ravines went off in three different directions.

Choosing the one he thought was right took Ben into and out of several box canyons. A maze of arroyos confronted him. They all looked promising at first, but led nowhere.

As the darkness increased, Ben switched on the headlights of the quad and followed a dimly seen, winding trail around the side of a hill. His sense of panic grew as he confronted a large rock blocking the path. His first thought was to make another U-turn, but a trail of rubble leading down to the stone made him reason that this was the correct trail after all. Perhaps his earlier passage had caused the rock to fall.

Ben's tired joints ached as he moved the heavy boulder out of the narrow pathway. The rock rolled down the slope and over the edge of a ravine. It smashed into the rusty sheet-metal wall of an old mine shack. The clanging sound rang out loudly, disturbing the night animals of the desert. A flock of bats uncoiled out of the abandoned shed, and a lone owl screeched. Chills ran down Ben's back.

The quad runner idled patiently. Ben hurried

around and got back on. He thought to himself about how dark it was and how the fuel was running low. He put the quad in gear, but something grabbed his attention. Off in the distance, a strange green glow grew in the night sky.

Maybe someone had come to rescue him, he thought. Ben headed down to the bottom of the incline, moving toward the light. The gleam increased in the sky ahead.

Suddenly the headlights of the quad flickered. They brightened, then dimmed, then increased again. The engine coughed, and the machine shuddered like an exhausted animal. Another chill crossed Ben's spine, and he abruptly changed his mind about going toward the mysterious light. At that moment the quad runner's engine sputtered, shook heavily, and died.

"Not now," he shouted aloud, pounding on the handlebars. "Not now!" Out in the dark expanse of desert, a glowing skeletal figure appeared, then vanished. Ben saw another skeleton, smaller than the first, then it too disappeared into thin air.



Ben was gripped with fear. He tried frantically to restart the engine. When his efforts failed, he got off and anxiously jiggled the wires, looking for something wrong but finding nothing he could repair.

Puffs of dust circled him like floating ghosts.

Ben crouched, trembling in terror, beside his machine. The ground began to rumble. A deep-pitched moaning noise, low at first, then increasing in volume, seemed to come from all directions at once.

The green glow was almost overhead, suddenly bathing him in a blinding light. The whole earth seemed to howl. Ben let out a scream, but there was no one to hear him. A rising storm of dust filled his eyes and clogged his breath. Backed up against his quad, he tried to run away, but there was nowhere to run—no escape at all.

# 4

The Last Chance Diner had been built in the fifties and had been well kept up by Grandma and Pop Fowler ever since. Inside, a horseshoe-shaped counter occupied the middle of the room. The stools circling the counter were round and covered with rose-colored vinyl. Each had a single row of brass studs around the edge.

To the left of the door was an old-style cash

register with a gum ball machine next to it. All along the walls were booths with seats covered in the same shade of pink as the stools. The entire diner, including the faded linoleum floor, was done in a combination of rose and baby blue.

The restaurant was filled with folks eating supper. Grandma Fowler was behind the counter making coffee and setting up for business in the late hours. When the coffee was brewing, she stepped out with a towel and wiped off the bar stools.

Mike sat across the counter from his mother, Gail Fowler. Winnie flanked him on one side and Spence on the other.

Mom examined the broken compass for a moment, then put it down beside Mike's plate. "I bet your grandpa'd be happy to take a look at that for you," she said gently.

Staring down at the shattered crystal, Mike murmured, "Thanks, Mom."



Gail Fowler studied her downcast son. "You OK?"

Mike's eyes met those of his mom. "Yeah," he said. "I—"

The bell on the diner's entry door jingled, announcing the arrival of another customer. Strolling in, Sheriff Smitty approached the counter. "Hello, Gail," Smitty said cheerfully. "Got any of that famous apple pie left?"

"Just sold the last piece, Smitty." Gail nodded toward Smitty's regular table where a generous slice of pie was already prepared. "Waiting for you."

"Thanks," Smitty said. He slid into his usual spot, and Grandma Fowler arrived with a fresh pot of coffee.

"Runnin' a little late tonight, aren't you, Sheriff?" Grandma filled Smitty's cup with the steaming, fragrant brew.

Smitty smiled when he replied, but his voice had a weary tone. "Yeah . . . we got a little investigation goin' on . . . not s'posed to talk about it."

Grandma Fowler set the coffeepot down on the table and said matter-of-factly, "You mean the burglary down at the cultural museum?"

Smitty's eyebrows arched in surprise, and a forkful of apple pie stopped halfway to his mouth. "I see the cat's already out of the bag."

Kate Fowler snorted. "The cat *ate* the bag." She unfolded a newspaper she had carried under her arm and spread it on the table so Smitty could read the headlines. In print large enough to be seen across the room, it announced "Museum Treasures Vanish."

Smitty's expression changed from surprise to

disgust as he read the words. "So much for . . . *top secret,"* he said with a shake of his head.

"Things don't just vanish," Grandma Fowler quizzed. "What's this all about?"

Frowning as if considering how much he should say, Smitty looked again at the newspaper account and then launched in. "Well, I've never seen anything quite like it. No windows were broken . . . no doors were forced. The alarm wasn't even set off. Weins, the curator, opened the place up, and the treasures were just . . . gone."

Mike, Winnie, and Spence exchanged interested looks. "Now there's a real case," Mike whispered.

Winnie nodded, but Mike noticed that her attention was divided between the sheriff's explanation and a stranger seated across the room. In contrast to the jeans and overalls of the townsfolk, the newcomer was dressed in city clothes.

Mike's grandmother continued to press for more information. "What treasures? I thought all the valuable stuff had been shipped off to the Smithsonian."



"Not all of it. . . . On top of that, some Aztec artifacts had just come in on loan from Mexico. Now they're gone too."

Kate's tone was sympathetic when she said, "Well, sounds like you got your work cut out for you."

"Not really. Those missing Aztec pieces make it an international incident." Smitty's drawl spread out the syllables of his last two words so that they captured the interest of everyone in the diner. "The FBI's moved in. . . . They claim it's their jurisdiction."

Winnie nudged Mike with her elbow and nodded toward the stranger. The man who looked like an accident lawyer on a TV commercial slopped some coffee out of his cup and rose hurriedly to go.

But Spence was also eager for Mike's attention. "Did you hear that?" Spence said, reacting with excitement to Smitty's last comment. "An international incident right here in Ambrosia!"

Mike licked his lips in anticipation. No more lost cats or missing false teeth for the Last Chance Detectives! "All right, all those in favor of taking on the museum robbery, say aye!" Spence joined him in an intense "Aye!" in which Winnie did not share. "Winnie," Mike asked. "What's wrong?"

She nodded again to indicate the stranger, now hurrying toward the exit. The skin of his angular face was stretched, and he had the appearance of someone in a terrible hurry to attend to some pressing business. As the stranger pushed open the door, Ben Jones rushed in under the man's arm.

"Outta my way! Outta my way!" Ben demanded urgently. Mike could see that his friend was covered with sweat and dirt. His face was streaked with grime, and his clothes were ripped in places. "Sheriff Smitty, am I glad to see you!" Ben said nothing to anyone else in the diner in his rush to Smitty's table.

In his slow, easy manner, Smitty took another sip of coffee and then said, "Howdy Ben. What's the . . ."

Ben grabbed the sheriff by the elbow. Mike was startled to see his friend so excited. "Ya gotta call the army! The National Guard! They're here!"

Ben's clutch jostled Smitty's cup, and some steaming coffee spilled on the sheriff's hand. "What in the blue blazes!" Smitty shouted. "Who?! Who's here?"

"The aliens! They're landing in the desert!"

Mike heard a momentary stunned silence in the diner. Here and there he saw shocked looks, while other faces showed raised eyebrows.



"They are!" Ben announced to the room.

Then it seemed that everyone was chuckling at once, a low wave of laughter that swept across the crowded room. A smile slowly formed on Smitty's face. "You almost had me goin' there for a minute."

"I'm not kidding!" Ben pleaded intensely. "Just

an hour ago . . . out there . . . a UFO turned off my quad runner and came at me with some kinda green Martian light!" Like a rising surf, the laughter bounced off one wall of the restaurant and swelled as it rushed back. It grew in volume till Ben had to shout to make himself heard. "I barely escaped with my life!"

Smitty detached the grip of Ben's stubby fingers from his shirtsleeve and said sternly, "All right, Ben. You've had your fun."

Sounding desperate to be believed, Ben begged, "Honest! A UFO! I saw it! You gotta believe me!" Mike exchanged a look of amazement with Winnie and Spence.

Smitty refolded his napkin and mopped the spilled coffee from the table. His voice was low at first as he addressed Ben. "Well, Ben, let's see. . . . Last time I heard you this excited was when you called and said old Mizz Tug was bein' robbed . . . saw a prowler go through her window, you said. . . . Only that was Mizz Tug herself 'cause she locked herself outta the house." The volume of the sheriff's words rose with retelling, and Ben seemed to shrink in size as he listened. "Here we come . . . all lights and sirens! Surround her house! Almost gave the poor lady a heart attack! So if you say the Martians are coming . . . I guess I better call the president himself!"

A tidal wave of renewed laughter rolled over the room. Mike saw that Ben's face was a contortion of anger and frustration, close to tears. "Yeah? Well, go ahead and laugh, but I'm telling the truth." Now the crowd was reacting to everything Ben said with gales of uproarious noise. In a voice as angry as Mike had ever heard his friend use, Ben said to Smitty, "If you were any kinda sheriff, you'd be out there looking for evidence 'stead of stuffing yourself with pie and getting fat!"

The mirth in the diner came to an abrupt and uncomfortable halt. Mike watched nervously to see how Smitty would react. "You'd best get on home, Ben," Mike heard the sheriff say. The words were soft but stern.

"I'm not going any—," Ben protested.

"Ben!" Smitty exploded. "You hear me? Straight home! I'll be callin' your folks to see that you did!"



Seeing Ben's head bowed in defeat, Mike watched as his friend retreated toward the door. Ben paused with his hand on the knob. He faced the group of Mike, Winnie, and Spence, but his eyes were locked on Mike's when he asked, "You guys believe me . . . don't you?"

The unbroken silence gave him the answer he did not want. Ben's shoulders sagged even farther as he shoved open the door and stumbled out of the diner. The sound of snickering chased him into the night, as folks repeated things Ben said and laughed all over again.

Winnie summed it up for the group when she said in a baffled voice, "The kid has totally lost it!"

# 5

Sticky from the desert's heavy morning dew, the tires on Mike's red BMX spit grass and sand as he pedaled. He pulled up to Pop's workshop, around the back of the hangar, and laid his bike down.

"Pop, are you in here?" Mike said, pushing the chipped white paint door open.

"Come on in, Mikey," a voice with a heavy southern accent instructed. It was Earl, lifelong friend since Pop's air force days and the best airplane mechanic the world had ever seen. "I think he's in the shop."

"Thanks, Earl," Mike said.

"You betcha."

"Over here, Mike," Pop called out, emerging from under the wing of a partly restored P-51 Mustang.

"Mom said that maybe you could fix my compass," Mike said, holding up the brass case.

"Sure," Pop said, taking the compass to his workbench. "Let's take a look. Hmmm . . . the crystal's busted."

"And Ben did it," Mike said in a disgusted tone.

Pop put the compass in a jeweler's vice, turned on a small work light, and examined it. "On purpose?" When Mike said nothing, Pop continued, "He made quite a scene last night . . . something about a UFO?"

Mike pulled a stool up to the table and sat down. "Yeah. Winnie says he just wanted attention after what he'd done, bein' such a jerk."

Pop stopped his work and studied Mike's expression. "You don't believe him?"

Mike hesitated a moment. "Come on, Pop. UFOs?"

"Yeah, pretty crazy," Pop agreed. "But Ben *thought* he saw something."

Mike shook his head. "He didn't see anything."

Pop put down his needle-nose pliers and switched off the light. "Engines are runnin' kinda rough, huh?"

Mike stared at him, trying to understand the phrase.

Pop went on, "An old saying we used to use when someone in the crew was feeling lousy. Rough engines can ground you. Y'know, keep you from completing your mission."

Mike, half smiling, understood. "More like fog on the runway and no place to land. Ben *was* my best friend. Now . . . I dunno."

"I know the feeling." Pop sat down on a stool next to Mike and crossed his arms. "Fog," he said, gazing off in the distance. Mike could almost see the memory roll across his grandfather's face. "A flyer's worst enemy. It covers every landmark. I remember one night we were headed out on a mission when, about eighty miles west of Paris, we were called back to base, and the fog was rolling in. Black as oil," he said, narrowing his eyes beneath bushy white eyebrows. "It covered every square inch of France. Both our side and the Nazi side too. No wonder we hadn't seen any enemy fighters. They figured the fog would kill us. Why even waste their bullets? If it hadn't been for the instruments, we wouldn't have been able to tell if we were upside down or right side up. It was pretty bad that night."

"What happened, Pop?"

Pop scratched his cheek, leaving a streak of grease on his face. "The control tower told us to fly till our fuel was gone, then ditch her." He clenched his teeth and his lips tightened. "Ditch the old gal and let her crash while we bailed out."

Mike licked his lips with anticipation. "What did you do?"

Pop paused a moment, his forehead creased with the recollection. "I stuck with the instruments . . . the compass and the rest. I stayed with the things that told me where the airfield had to be."

"Go on," Mike said anxiously. "What happened?"

"East to west I made my first pass, then another the other direction. There was no wind to move the fog . . . no sign that any one heavy dark mass was any different than another. I kept prayin'. The instruments showed that the landing strip was right there, only I couldn't see it."

Mike leaned forward, staring at his grandfather. His eyes were wide and his mouth open. "And then what?"

"Well, on the third pass, I told the crew to get

braced, we were goin' in. The flaps were down and the gear locked. The fuel was runnin' on reserve, and I looked down—" Pop closed his eyes as the memory overwhelmed him—"and there were the runway lights, clear as anything. It was like God reached out his hand and scooped out a big place for us to land. And we set her down, bingo, on the money."

"Wow," Mike said, looking down at the floor and considering the miracle.

"Mike," Pop said, reaching out his strong, weathered hand and putting it on Mike's shoulder, "life is full of rocky times, and sometimes you feel lost or confused about things that happen—or about other people. But the point is, the Lord knows where you are and what's goin' on, even when you can't see your hand in front of your face. Do you understand what I mean?" Pop asked seriously.

"Yeah, I think so. You're saying I should follow what I know is true and not depend on my feelings."

"Bingo," Pop said, nodding. "You know, you have another compass that your dad gave you."

Mike looked confused, then said, "You mean the Bible?" He took the small Bible out of his pocket to show Pop. "What's it got to say about situations like, you know, Ben and me?"

Pop motioned for the Bible, which Mike handed to him. As he flipped through the worn pages to the book of Ephesians, Pop answered, “Well, for one thing, it says a friend sticks closer than a brother. But here, read this.”

Mike took the Bible from Pop and read aloud to where his grandfather’s finger was pointing. “Be kind to each other, tenderhearted, forgiving one another, just as God has forgiven you because you belong to Christ.”

There was silence while Mike considered the words. “I see you’re thinking about what that means to you and Ben,” Pop said. “Just follow the Compass, and you’ll be fine.” He turned back to the brass case full of shards of broken glass. “And don’t worry about this. The face may be broken, but it’ll work again. You hang on to it till I get another crystal. OK?” Pop handed Mike the compass. “Now run along and have fun.”

Mike placed the instrument back on his belt. “Thanks, Pop. See ya later,” he called out, running off through the hangar.



“Mike, come here!” Winnie urged as Mike climbed in through the bottom hatch of the B-17. “You’ve got to see this. It’s amazing!”

“Boy, it’s hot out there,” Mike said, wiping

his face with the back of his hand. Then, pulling up a chair, he questioned, "OK, what's going on?"

"You're never going to believe this! Spencer's an absolute genius."

Mike chuckled, "Absolute genius? I thought he was just borderline genius. Aren't you just borderline genius, Spence?"

"Yeah, I'm getting that way from hanging around you guys." Spencer smiled as he typed on his small but powerful Macintosh PowerBook.

Mike scooted his chair closer and peered over Spencer's shoulder. "So what am I looking at here?" Mike asked.

Winnie leaned across from the other side of Spence. She pointed a slender finger at the screen. "The museum-robbery case! This is the actual floor plan of the place."

Mike's eyes lit up, and he sat back in his chair. "The floor plan to the museum? Spence, is this legal?"



Spencer looked up at the ceiling. "Of course," he said in a reassuring tone. "I simply accessed the public library's computer files, found the city's architectural records, and downloaded the museum's blueprint onto my computer."

"Spence, you're an absolute genius," Mike agreed, nodding his head and grinning.

Spencer turned back to his computer. The blue

screen lit up his face and made glowing round reflections in his glasses. "OK, here's what we've got. It's a single-story building made up of about seven separate rooms. All doors and windows are marked." He gestured toward the screen. "This is the lobby, the gift shop, three main display rooms, and a small shipping dock. It's a pretty basic layout."

Mike rested his chin on his hand. "And there was no sign of forced entry," he said, baffled.

"The paper reported that the security system is state of the art. Nobody could get in or out through the doors or windows without being detected," Winnie announced.

"What are these small rooms?" Mike asked, indicating a group of small squares on the face of the monitor.

"These two are probably bathrooms," Spencer said, squinting. "And the other is . . . some kind of closet." He enlarged the image on his screen as if zooming in with a telescope. "No, wait a minute . . . it's a staircase," he concluded with surprise.

"But I've been there. It's a single-story building," Winnie said.

Mike frowned in deep concentration. Suddenly he snapped his fingers as realization struck him. "Of course . . . a basement!"

The other two looked at him thoughtfully, considering the possibility.

"Give me a second," Spencer said, tapping his chin with his finger. "There's one more screen I haven't tried." His nimble fingers made a series of rapid keystrokes.

Mike turned to Winnie. "If there is some other way into that basement, the burglars could have gotten in there."

Spencer pulled up the new display on the computer. "You got one thing right. There is a basement, but unfortunately, there are no doors or windows."

Winnie patted Mike on the back. "Sorry, Mike. Good try though."

Ben's voice drifted up through the hatch, but the boy did not enter the clubhouse. "Mike," he called in a shaky tone. "Mike, can I talk to you?"

Mike looked from Winnie to Spence. "Be right out," he yelled. Then to the other two detectives he added, "Keep working on it. . . . There may be some investigating for us to do yet."

Outside the B-17, Ben stood in the shade of the wing until Mike dropped from the hatch and joined him. Mike saw that Ben had two muddy streaks down his face that looked like tearstains.

Ben plopped down on the ground. After an awkward moment, Mike sat on Ben's left.

Mike pulled out the broken compass and looked at it. Ben was still staring at his shoes and did not notice. Setting the compass behind him where neither he nor Ben could see it, Mike turned to his friend. "I know you feel bad," Mike said after a long pause.

Ben sighed heavily, but said nothing. Mike saw his lips move, forming the word *sorry.*

"No one believes me when I say that I know my dad is still alive somewhere," Mike added.

"I believe it, Mike," Ben said. "I believe it 'cause you do." He paused. "I know I was a jerk yesterday. . . . And I'm awful sorry about your compass."

"It's OK," Mike said. "Pop says he can fix it."

Ben nodded, wiping his dirty face with the back of his hand. "I'm glad. But you gotta believe me about the rest. I'm not making it up. . . . Honest. I've told whoppers before, but not this time. If you'll just go out there with me, you'll see."

"OK, it's a deal," Mike said. "Friends believe in each other, right?"

"Right," Ben said brightening. "You'll see, Mike. Really."

Mike raised his hand for the Last Chance

salute. Ben lifted his hand also, and the two gave each other a high five, purposely missing and barking once like a seal.

"Come on, buddy," Mike said. "We've got some thinking to do!"

# 6

The shiny walls of the B-17 glimmered in the hot sun. Inside their clubhouse, the Last Chance Detectives were spread out from the cockpit to the tail section.

"Running lights on," Mike commanded from high up in the pilot's seat.

"Lights on," echoed Winnie. She sat in the copilot's seat next to Mike.

In the tail section of the plane, Ben lay on the dusty floor, staring at the screen of the TV/VCR. "Mike," he shouted. "Come here! This is a great movie." When he got no reply, Ben whined, "Mike, it's *The Day the Earth Stood Still!* You're gonna miss the best part!"

Mike's voice drifted back from the cockpit, "I'm busy landing this plane."

Occasional buzzing, popping, and hissing could be heard from the radio halfway down the fuselage near the bomb-bay doors. Spencer sat in the radioman's seat, quietly scanning the dial and gently adjusting the knobs. Having set aside the museum robbery, he was searching for another of the mysterious signals.

"Oh man, did you see that freaky light from the robot's eye?" Ben shouted. "It was just like the one I saw last night." He shivered at the thought.

Mike shook his head and looked at Wynona with a raised eyebrow. "Flaps down."



Wynona pulled the stiff black lever in the center of the instrument panel. "You know, Mike, there are a lot of Navajo legends about the mesas."

Mike pushed a few buttons. "Anything like the lights Ben says he—" He stopped in midsentence. "I mean the lights Ben saw?"

Mike and Winnie turned around to see if Ben heard. He had not; he was too zeroed in on the strange sounds from the spaceship on the television.

"Not exactly," Winnie replied, "but the elders say that there are evil places in the desert."

Spencer looked up momentarily from his work. "Some of your people still believe those legends?"

Wynona shrugged. "I heard from some of my father's friends that they have seen flickering white spirits that danced in the dark and disappeared before their eyes." She paused for a moment. "I don't know how much they really believe, but I know that there are some canyons they won't go near after dark."

Ben suddenly stood up. "Man, why didn't I have a video camera with me? I could have been rich and famous. I can see it now." Running forward to stand just behind the cockpit, he addressed the group, waving an imaginary newspaper and pointing to an imaginary headline. "'Ambrosia Youth Contacts Aliens.' I could have been famous!"

"You could have sold it to *Amazing Stories,*" Mike added.

Winnie added, "I guess you fell into a barrel of jellybeans with your mouth sewn up. It's an old Chinese proverb."

"Chinese?!" snickered Mike and Ben, looking puzzled.

The conversation was interrupted by a loud, sticky popping from the radio, followed by the same creepy, raspy voice. *"Ezeerck . . . ska-nah-nah-nah . . . um-sadatt. . . ."* The four friends sat silently listening. The radio message faded out, leaving behind an eerie sounding hiss.

"Good job, Spence! It looks like your work paid off," congratulated Mike. "You found it again!"

Ben asked, "Will you guys go with me to find my quad?"

"I don't know, Ben. You don't want a headline that reads, 'Ambrosia Youth Captured by Aliens,'" Winnie said.

Mike stood up and took charge. "We actually have three mysteries now: the museum theft, what Ben saw, and the radio messages. Maybe they are connected somehow and maybe not. Either way, Ben needs to recover his quad. We'll go with you, Ben, to Smitty's, but I think we should go see if Pop will come with us to check out the museum."



The door of the sheriff's office creaked loudly as the four Last Chance Detectives piled into the sheriff's tiny headquarters located in the center of town. The light green walls were covered with wanted posters. On one was the name Roger Cantonelli. It said he was wanted by the FBI.

To the right side of the office, behind a wooden counter topped with piles of papers and the black box of a CB radio, sat Smitty's wife, Arlene. She was plump, with bright red hair, and was as loud and cheerful as Smitty was quiet.

"Hi, guys! Is everybody all right? Ben, how are you after last night's little adventure?" Arlene asked in her high-pitched voice.

Ben nodded, but remembered the previous night's ridicule. Afraid to say anything, he looked at the floor.

Winnie spoke up, "We'd like to see Sheriff Smitty, please."

"It's official business," Spencer added.

Looking very surprised, Arlene said, "Well, of course. I'll just call the sheriff." She flipped the toggle of the tan intercom. A shrill buzzing could be heard from behind the closed door of the inner office. "Smitty, you have citizens out here who need your help."

"I'll be right out," the box squawked in reply. Mike could hear the sound of Smitty's chair creaking and his boots slapping the floor. Soon the frosted-glass door in the back of the office opened, and Smitty appeared. "Hello, kids." He looked at Ben. "You don't look quite so pale today as you did last night," he said with a chuckle. "What can I do for you?"

Ben did not bother to raise his head but, instead, edged toward the door.

Mike stepped in. "It's about the quad runner, sir."

"You said you'd help Ben bring it back," Wynona added.

Spencer spoke up, "Besides, sir, we thought you might like to investigate the strange occurrence that Ben reported."

Smitty laughed from deep in his chest. "Ben's strange occurrence has more to do with reading too many comic books and eating too much Rocky Road ice cream at bedtime. Now how's that for a . . ." He stopped in midthought when he caught Arlene's disapproving stare. "OK, OK. It's a quiet day anyhow. Is there anything on the books?" he asked Arlene.



"Just this envelope that came for you," she answered, handing him a manila folder. On it, Mike caught a glimpse of the address, labeled in red. Above Smitty's name it said FBI-Classified.

"I'll read it when I get back." Smitty turned to the kids. "Meet me outside in five minutes, and we'll go see if we can round up a little lost quad runner."

Outside Sheriff Smitty's office, in Ambrosia's one and only main street, the Last Chance Detectives stood close together, talking in low tones. "It's hopeless. He thinks I'm a loony tune. Probably the whole town thinks so too," Ben said to the group, looking very defeated.

Mike put his hand on Ben's shoulder. "C'mon, don't take it so hard. He just needs proof, that's all."

"Evidence," Spencer said. "Cold hard facts."

Ben had a tiny glimmer of hope in his eye. "Are you guys saying you believe me now?"

"The mesa *is* creepy, Ben," Wynona agreed. "I don't know what you saw out there, but I'm sure you saw something."

"Hmm," Spencer put his hand on his chin. "And when one is faced with new phenomena, one must seek further facts before forming a hypothesis."

"What's that mean?" Ben said, looking puzzled.

Spencer cocked his head to the side. "It means show me."

Mike looked thoughtfully at Ben. "If Sheriff Smitty could see what you saw, then the whole rest of the town would believe too, right?"

"But it's daylight now. There's nothing to see," Ben noted. His arms hung at his sides while he scuffed the dirt with the toe of his sneaker.

"Hey," Mike said, punching Ben in the shoulder. "Broad daylight? How's this for an idea? Don't go straight for the quad, see? Wander around like you're looking for it till about the same time as last night. Then head off in the direction you went. Maybe, just maybe, whatever happened will show up again."

"I dunno. Maybe it isn't worth it. What if I just barely escaped being captured by something with big sharp teeth and long claws?" Mike could tell that his friend was half interested and half scared.

Winnie slapped Ben on the head. "Wake up! You're not gonna be alone this time. Sheriff Smitty wouldn't let anything happen."

"OK then, it's a plan," Mike announced. "While you're getting your quad, we'll head to the museum. And Ben—why not take your camera?"

At that Ben smiled and took his camera out of his book bag. "Already thought of it."



The door of the sheriff's office opened, and Smitty emerged with a gas can. "All right, let's go see if we can locate that quad."

The four kids exchanged glances. Mike nodded his confirmation of their plan, though he felt a twinge of guilt for intending to trick the sheriff.

"Meet you back at the plane tonight, Ben." Mike gave his friend a pat on the back as Ben climbed into the pickup.

# 7

It was already late afternoon before Smitty and Ben set out to find the stranded quad. The sun was sinking behind the mesas, framing them against a deep red-orange glow in the sky. A cool wind drifted across the vast landscape.

Mike, Spencer, and Winnie were probably on their way to the museum by now, Ben thought as he sat silently beside Smitty. Smitty's patrol truck rattled and squeaked with each rut they bounced through. The constant noise, lasting for a couple hours, wore on Ben's already fragile nerves.

*Why am I here?* he thought to himself. *I could have been killed last night, and now I come back!* "Stupid!" he said aloud, slapping himself in the forehead.

"What?" Smitty asked. "Are you lost again?"

"Oh, uh . . . no, sir, this is the way. . . . I'm sure of it, I think." Ben looked out the window and wished Mike was in the truck. "Although . . . ," Ben said as if he was not quite sure. Smitty slammed on the brakes.

"Are you sure you didn't fall and bump your head out here? We've spent hours—and it'll be dark soon." Ben looked over the mesa and tried to estimate how much light they had left as Smitty switched on his headlights.

Ben recognized the knoll where the group had argued and split up the day before. "If we don't find that quad soon," Smitty said, "it's going to have to sit out here and rust for a few more—"



"Oh, we'll find it."

"Well, it's getting on dinnertime."

Ben pulled out a melted Butterfinger candy bar and offered half to Smitty. "Uh . . . Sheriff Smitty, sir?"

"Uh-huh?"

"I just wanted to apologize for what I said last night . . . the thing about the pie. But I'm still sticking to my story."

"Is that why you brought that thing?" Smitty pointed to the camera.

"Yeah. You know. . . . Just in case."

"Well, you probably just ran out of gas. You sure this is the right direction?"

"I think so, sir. Over that way, sir," Ben said innocently.

Smitty gradually made the course change to follow the rise where the dirt changed color from the sandy brown into the rust color that the mesas carried. They continued on toward the hill and the canyon where Ben had abandoned the quad. The last light in the west was a dim muddy red.

Time passed in the darkness with Smitty muttering remarks under his breath about imaginary spacemen. At last he stopped on the brow of a steep hill and pointed down a slope. Reaching the spot, Smitty turned on his searchlight and angled it down the hill. Ben saw his quad, sitting just where he had left it the night before.

"Well, there's your machine—guess the spacemen didn't want it," Smitty joked.

Turning the truck to angle across the hill, Smitty drove the truck down the slope and stopped next to the quad. Ben felt his heartbeat quicken as Smitty opened the door and got out. The sheriff left the engine running and the lights on so he could see what he was doing at the quad.

Smitty leaned over the controls and turned the key in the ignition. As Ben looked on, it started right up, and in the glare of the headlights, he saw a look of surprise cross Smitty's face.

"Told you it wasn't out of gas," Ben yelled over the engine noise. His heart was pounding in his ears as he stared out into the darkness beyond the headlights. Ben was sweating, and he found it refreshing when a strong breeze picked up and blew through the open windows of the cab of the truck.

The headlights faded to a yellow tint, then they came back up to full brightness again. Smitty noticed and shouted, "Ben, don't you touch anything in that truck!"

"But I . . . ," Ben started to say. He raised both of his hands to show he was not touching anything. Then the lights dimmed once more, this time for a long time, then flared up again.

Smitty had just left the quad and stomped toward his truck when Ben heard a low howl begin, and the velocity of the breeze increased. The swirl of air was suddenly not pleasant. "The wind!" Ben yelled just before the headlights dimmed a final time and the engine died. So did the engine of the quad. "Last night . . . the wind!"

A green glow lit the ridge above them. Behind it, Ben could only make out the silhouette of an oval shape. Its movement was fluid and eerie, sliding in a half circle in the sky around them as if examining them. It swung around the cab of the truck, and a brilliant beam shone directly into Ben's eyes. The inner ring of the light was bright white with the outside a glistening blue. It left Ben seeing purple spots. He raised the camera and screamed, "They're blinding us! We can't see and they'll eat us!"

The circle of light that the beam projected onto the ground swung back around the truck and stopped on Smitty and the now silent quad. It grew in intensity as Smitty froze and stared straight up at it. "Go!" he yelled at Ben. "Go! Get out of here!"

Popping open the door of the truck in a burst of terror, Ben half jumped and half fell, tumbling to the rocky soil. He scrambled toward the quad. Ben fell once and looked back to see Smitty backed against the truck, shielding his eyes with both arms in the air. As Ben struggled to reach the quad, he imagined some huge invisible monster that Smitty was trying to fight.

Ben leapt onto his quad, and the engine sputtered once; then he roared away toward the top of the hill.

Still clutching his camera, Ben did not even look back as he sped through the desert toward Ambrosia.

Mike, Spence, and Winnie all sat crammed into the cab of Pop's '54 Chevy pickup truck as Pop drove them over the dark highway toward the museum.

"We sure appreciate this, sir," Spence said to Pop.

"No need to thank me yet," Pop replied. "I'm not even sure if the museum is still open."

Winnie joined in the conversation. "But if it is, do you really think you can get us in?"

"Well," Pop said, "I can't make any promises, but old Weins and I have been friends for years, and—"



At that moment the form of a quad runner entered the beam of the headlights. It roared straight for the truck! Pop shouted and swerved off the road, narrowly missing the quad and its driver.

"What . . . ?"

Pop leaned forward and peered through the darkness. "Why it looks like—"

*"Ben!"* Mike shouted.

"He's headed for the sheriff's station," Winnie cried.

"Something's wrong for sure." Pop pointed the truck to follow Ben.

"Smitty, do you read me? Smitty, this is Arlene. Come in, please. Why don't you answer? Over." Arlene's voice squeaked into the CB radio on the counter of the sheriff's office. Around her stood the four kids, as well as Pop Fowler, Mike's mom, and a handful of other concerned townspeople.

The chatter of voices momentarily stopped as everyone strained to listen for a reply. There was none—only the empty hiss of static. The babble of speculation erupted again.

Pop glanced at Ben. "Ben! This is no time for games. Are you sure about all of this?"

"Honest, Pop! I wouldn't worry Arlene like this for no reason. And now Smitty's seen it too! You'll see!"

"Maybe Smitty's wrecked the truck, trying to get away from whatever it was!" said Mike.

"We should call the National Guard!"

"The air force!"

From behind him, Ben tapped Mike on the

shoulder. "It's just like *Invasion of Planet Earth!* It was the strangest thing I've ever witnessed," said Ben.

Winnie squinted and said, "All the old legends—"

"Smitty! Come in, Smitty!" Arlene cried, her voice running up to an even higher pitch in her anxiety.

The group listened again, leaning toward the radio as if the concentration of their willpower could make Smitty respond. Only the fuzzy sound of hollow air filled the little room, and then . . .

"It's OK, Arlene. . . . I'm on the way in now. Over." Smitty's tone was calm and reassuring.

"What's happening out there?" Arlene asked. "I've been worried sick."

There was a long pause. The citizens of Ambrosia filled the wait with an exchange of questioning looks.

"Uh, nothing really. We found the quad and—"

Smitty's explanation was cut off by Arlene. "Smitty, Ben's here. He said the engine died and the light came again and—"

Sounding very official, the sheriff replied, "Arlene, this channel is for official business only, not gossip. Everything here is under control. My ETA is three-zero minutes. Smitty out."

Many of the adults looked angry while others were puzzled. Mike looked at each of his fellow detectives in turn. On each face he read alarm and confusion. What did Smitty mean?

Arlene spoke up sternly. "Did you ever hear of the boy who cried wolf?"

Ben became angry. "But I did tell the truth! We both saw the light. Smitty saw it too! It froze the truck engine, and he yelled for me to get away, to go for help."

Arlene stood angrily and pointed to the door. "Out!" she ordered.

Ben's face was streaked with tears when Mike approached him. "You must think I'm a lunatic." Ben sniffed.

"No, Ben . . . I don't," Mike said quietly.

"But you don't believe me."

"I'm not sure what to believe, Ben. But I do know that I believe in you. You're my best friend, and yesterday with the compass . . . I never should have treated you like that. I'm sorry." Mike shook hands with Ben.

"What about the others?" Ben asked.

"I don't know. If only you had some proof."

Ben brightened at that, and he snapped his fingers as he remembered something. "My camera!" he shouted happily.



That night, back on the B-17, Winnie worked to develop the film from Ben's camera. In a curtained-off area of the plane, she stood with a scowl on her face as Mike and Spence looked on in the glow of the red light.

"I can't believe you guys are falling for this again," she snapped.

Ben stuck his head through the curtain to check the progress. "Just you wait, Winnie! You'll see!"

"Ben!" Spence warned. "You're letting the light in!"

"Sorry," Ben apologized. "Can you make out anything yet?"

Spencer leaned closer. "It's just beginning to develop."

Winnie stood with her arms crossed. She did not believe that anything would show up at first, but then an image began to appear.

"Something's happening!" Ben said in an excited voice.

"Sure enough!" Mike agreed.

"What!" Winnie was suddenly caught up in the excitement. "Can you see it? Did it turn out?"

"Yep!" Spence said with a smile. "It's a great picture of Ben's finger!"

A groan rose up. The picture at first glance seemed ruined. But then Mike looked closer. "Hold on." Mike held it up. Ben's finger doesn't block the whole shot. . . . What's this around it?"

The detectives crowded closer. Spence pulled

out a magnifying glass. “Hmmmmm. That could be a light source in the top corner.”

Mike agreed. “And look at the way it fans out at the bottom.”

Ben was relieved. “I told you I wasn’t making it up!”

“But what about Smitty?” Mike sighed and shook his head. “Why isn’t he telling what he saw?” This seemed the biggest mystery of all to Mike.

# 8

The Last Chance Detectives sat on the steps of the diner with Cokes. Mike was on the top landing, tapping a thoughtful rhythm on the soda can. Winnie and Spence sprawled in uncomfortable silence. On the bottom tread, Ben stared at the dirt and sometimes lashed out with his foot at a pebble. Even Pop's old dog lay by the side of the steps, seeming dismal and depressed.

"I wonder why he . . . ," Ben started for the fifteenth time.

"Don't wonder," Mike said. "Smitty's a good guy. Nothing we can think of makes sense. It's just not like him."

Then the group sat quiet again. Winnie raised her hand to the afternoon sun, and Mike did the same, trying to see what she was looking at. A truck was coming down the road, looking odd and thin in the heat waves coming off of the pavement. Then Mike recognized the emergency lights on top: It was Smitty.

The kids watched as Smitty rolled to a stop in the gas station and got out to fill his tank.

"There's the traitor," Mike said.

"Yeah," added Winnie, "the traitor."

"The eggs Benedict of Ambrosia," Ben remarked. Mike rolled his eyes.

"I believe you mean Benedict Arnold," corrected Spencer. He was cleaning his glasses as the others stood and walked toward the gas pump. "You know," Spencer said, "I believe now would be an excellent time to confront Mr. . . ." Reaching back, Mike grabbed Spencer and jerked him to his feet.



The row of Last Chance Detectives formed a single-minded rank as they approached Smitty's truck in gunfighter formation. As they neared the sheriff's vehicle, they heard the soft noise of the truck radio.

"So c'mon to Western Bill's where everybody's a cowboy," the radio announcer finished. It then started to play the theme song of *The Good, the Bad and the Ugly.* Out of the corner of his eye Mike caught a glimpse of Ben swaggering like Clint Eastwood and whistling along with the music.

Operating the fuel pump on the side of the truck with his back to the kids, Smitty at last noticed them moving toward him. He looked up and instantly reached in the open window to shut off the radio. The gunfighter music stopped, and about ten feet separated him from the angry Last Chance Detectives.

There was an awkward silence until Spence said, "Why did you do it, sir?"

"Ben looks like a crybaby," Winnie said.

Then Ben added, "Say it ain't so, Joe!" which earned him a slap on the head from Winnie. Then there was silence again as Smitty chewed his gum and thought of an answer.

"I didn't do anything," he said. "And I don't want you kids out there anymore. That whole area is riddled with mine shafts, and if one of you fell in one—" He walked forward and spoke directly to Ben—"I don't want to spend my free time fishing you out. Now, if I hear of you kids going out there, I'll . . . I'll tell your parents, or I'll lock you up for trespassing. Now run along and play."

"Sir," Mike said, "I *don't* understand." A look of concern narrowed Smitty's eyes, but he offered no further explanation.

Walking back to the steps of the diner, the four friends stood and watched in a kind of a daze. Smitty went into the station and paid, then drove off without another word.

"How could he say he—," Winnie started.

"It doesn't matter," Mike said. "There's something going on that he's not telling, and we'll find out our way!"

The Last Chance Detectives huddled in the B-17 over their map of the area around Ambrosia.

"OK, guys," Mike said, "listen up. We were about two miles southeast of Navajo Mesa." He tapped his finger down onto the map. "Right about here . . . close to the rock called Tall Leader when—"

"You know, guys," Ben cut in, "I've been thinking."

"Wow," said Winnie. "A new experience for you."

"Cool it," Ben said. "This is serious. Maybe

that really was a spaceship . . . and maybe they brainwashed Sheriff Smitty. That's why he's not admitting—or can't remember—what happened! Making a slave out of Smitty is the first step in their plan to take over Ambrosia!"

"Take over Ambrosia?" Winnie asked with a giggle. "Why?"

"I don't believe that the sheriff would remember us if his thought processes had been altered," Spencer said. "Besides, everyone knows that brainwashed people talk in a very monotone voice, as if stripped of all personality."

"Yeah, Ben," Mike said. "Spencer's right. I think whatever's going on is linked to those weird radio signals."

"Bet you're right," Wynona agreed.

"It would be highly unlikely otherwise," Spencer said. "Perhaps we should mention the transmissions to the sheriff."

"Not now!" Mike said. "We can't. If only we had a way to find out where the broadcast was coming from, we wouldn't need the sheriff at all."

"It might be possible," Spencer said thoughtfully. "Have any of you noticed me working on the Omega receiver?"

"Is that the latest Nintendo game?" Ben asked excitedly. Winnie aimed another slap at Ben's head, but he expected it and ducked out of the way.

"No, it's a navigation device," Spencer said. "Like the radio, it works on very low frequency. I easily modified it to lock on to the mystery signal and pinpoint the origin of the transmission."

"Seriously?" Mike asked. "Like a direction finder?"

"Right," Spencer said. "And it's ready to go."

"What are we waiting for?" Winnie asked.

"Have you almost got it?" Winnie asked impatiently.

"He'll get it," Mike assured her.

Mike, Winnie, and Ben sat in a circle around Spence on the floor plates of the B-17 as he continued to work on the Omega receiver.

"You've been working on it for hours," Ben noted.

"Chill out, Ben, and he'll get done a lot sooner," Mike said with irritation.

Spencer placed a nine-volt battery inside the contraption that was part radio dial, part wooden box, and part antenna wire bent into a loop the shape of an oversize lightbulb. A cable leading to a pair of earphones dangled from the back. From the look of concentration on Spence's face, Mike could tell how much his new friend wanted to succeed, wanted to prove his value as the newest Last Chance Detective.



Ben groaned, "But I'm hungry and—" His complaint was cut off in midsentence by a crackling sound that came from the modified Omega receiver. This sound was followed by a high-pitched whine, like the shrill of a giant mosquito.

Mike's excitement was too much for even him to hold in. "Is it working?"

"Shhh!" Spencer said raising his hand for silence.

*"Segurro . . . extensor,"* a voice from the radio crackled.

Spencer sat with a faraway look, staring off toward a vacant corner of the plane. While the others watched with anticipation, he turned the knobs laboriously, his nimble fingers hard at work. A clicking sound came from the earphones, and the needle of a lighted dial swung up and down its scale.

*"Merto . . . seeplay,"* the rasping tone said, the signal wandering in and out of focus. Silence fell over the group. Spencer flipped a switch and adjusted another thumb wheel and the static was gone. With three pairs of eyes watching him intently, he turned to the group and announced, "I've got it!"

Cheers of excitement and congratulations erupted from the group. Mike nodded in satisfaction. Spencer was a great new addition to the group, and with their radio direction finder working, the Last Chance Detectives were on their way!

# 9

Dust, thick with the stale smell of old, rotting timbers, rose from the dark hole. Ben stood close to the edge, his back to the mine shaft.

"Is this right?" Mike asked.

"The Omega says it is," Spencer replied.

Ben said nervously, "Great, Mike, great. . . . OK, we found it, now let's get out of here."

Mike looked at Ben with disbelief. "You can't be serious."

Spencer squinted and took a step toward Ben. "We came out here to obtain evidence to support our contention. So far, all we've discovered is a hole in the ground."

"And it's just like a hundred other old mines. Grandma says most of them never amounted to anything," Winnie noted.

Mike looked around him. Off in the distance was a low hill; beside that, the entrance to another box canyon. Aside from those landmarks, all that was in view was the hole in the ground and miles of empty desert. "Nobody's been here," he said in a disappointed tone. "No tracks, no footprints. There's no signs at all."

Wynona looked up thoughtfully. "'Course, the main tunnel would prob'ly come out somewhere over that way." She pointed in the direction of the canyon.

"That must be it!" Mike clenched his fist. "A different way in," he said positively.



Spencer turned the dials on the black box. "The Omega still shows we're on the right spot."

Mike looked at the others and said, "We're onto something here! Let's go find the entrance."

"Hold on a minute." Ben put his hands up in protest. "Hasn't anybody 'cept me noticed that it's gonna be dark soon?" Carelessly he took a step back, placing his foot on a rock near the edge of the shaft. "I say we get out of here before something hap—"

The rock under Ben's foot rolled loose. He tumbled toward the edge, making a futile attempt to grab hold of a clump of brush. Gravel and dirt slid past him into the dark hole. Mike dove to grasp Ben's arm, but it was too late. The handful of weeds ripped free, and Ben disappeared, wailing for help, into the depths of the dark shaft.

"Ben! Ben!" Mike called frantically. "Can you hear me? Are you all right?"

There was no answer. Winnie and Spencer stood frozen with fear.

"Hold on to my legs," Mike shouted.

Winnie and Spencer held tightly to Mike's legs as he got down on his stomach. He crawled cautiously over to the edge and looked in.

"Can you see him?" Winnie cried.

"No, but I think I can make out the bottom of the shaft. It's only fifteen feet down," Mike answered, relieved that the drop was not further.



Spotting an old ladder upright on the other side of the hole, Mike ordered, "Quick, pull me back. There's a ladder. I'm gonna go down and help him."

A lump formed in Mike's throat with the worry he felt for Ben. Winnie and Spencer pulled Mike back from the edge, and he circled the danger of the pit.

Dusk arrived with the sinking sun. An early evening breeze kicked up the dust. Mike quickly made his way to the ladder. As Winnie and Spence watched him, their silhouettes cast long shadows over the red earth.

"Wait here. I'll go see how bad he's hurt," Mike instructed.

"Is it safe?" Spencer asked as Mike took his first step on the decayed rung of the rickety ladder. "What about termites?"

"I think it's OK," Mike said softly. He took another step. The old board creaked and sagged with his weight. He paused there a moment. "Slowly, slowly," he whispered to himself, trying to stay calm. Gently he picked up his foot again, placing it on the rung below.

"Be careful, Mike," Winnie called.

"I will," Mike replied, his hands clenching the rough wood of the uprights. "These boards are strong enough to hold me."



A loud cracking sound echoed from the pit. Mike's arms flung backward as he dropped.

Hitting the bottom with a hollow thud, dust billowed up under his feet. Mike landed with a grunt.

Winnie screamed and covered her face with her hands.

"Mike!" Spencer yelled.

"I'm all right," Mike's voice called out from below. "I landed feet first," he said, brushing himself off.

"What do you see?" Winnie asked. "Where's Ben?"

"It's too dark," Mike said, gazing up at the faces of Winnie and Spence framed in the opening above him. "Throw me the flashlight."

Moments later, Spencer's arm appeared over the edge, light in hand. "I'm ready," Mike said. "Drop it." Then after Mike caught the flashlight and looked around, he said, "There's a tunnel down—Ahh!" he yelled when something grabbed him from behind.

Turning quickly around, Mike saw with relief that it was only Ben. "Why didn't you answer me? We thought you were killed," Mike said angrily.

Ben stood panting. "Knocked the wind out of me."

"I'm glad you're all right," Mike said, grasping Ben's arm. But he shook his head when he studied the broken ladder. "We'll never get out this way. Winnie," he called upward, "you and Spence go to the main entrance and wait for us. If we don't come in thirty minutes, or if you see anything . . . strange . . . go get Sheriff Smitty."

"OK," Winnie answered. "You be careful."

Ben looked unhappy. "Strange?" he said. "Like how strange? Couldn't we make it fifteen minutes? Better yet, ten?"

Mike pulled Ben's arm. "Let's go, Ben," he commanded, as they walked off into the eerie darkness, following the tunnel of the old abandoned mine.

"Are you sure the entrance is down here?" Spence asked. He and Winnie wandered through the box canyon east of the shaft Mike and Ben had fallen into. So far, they had found no trace of a tunnel, no indication of humans at all.

Winnie sighed, "There's got to be. Mines almost always have a side entrance so they can move the ore out on tracks."

"Maybe it caved in due to natural erosion," Spencer pondered aloud, "or maybe it was sealed shut with dynamite so no one could get lost in it."

"But not if this mine is the hideout we think it is," Winnie pointed out. "Nobody could go in and out using only the shaft Mike and Ben went down."

The distant rumble of an engine reached their ears. "Come on, Spence! Somebody's comin'," Winnie urged. She scrambled up the side of the hill in search of a hiding place. Spencer hurried to follow. His short legs kicked red rocks and dirt clods loose, but he made no progress up an overhanging bank.

"I can't make it," he said, hanging on the edge by his elbows.

Turning back to help, Winnie reached down and grabbed him. As she did so, the lights of the approaching vehicle struck the closest bend of the canyon as it neared them.

"There they are," Winnie yelled, dragging Spencer up and behind a pile of brush. His glasses were crossways on his face, and the knees of his pants had suddenly acquired rips, but he was out of sight just in time.

The vehicle rounded the corner of the dry wash and slowed just below them. It was a black, steel-caged, four-seater desert Odyssey, with two men inside and a strange purple light on the front. The light shone ahead, revealing a mysteriously glowing skeletal figure painted on the rocks of the canyon wall. The stick figure held its arms in the air, in perfect mimic of the gesture *STOP,* and the Odyssey parked right in front of it.

As Winnie and Spence watched with amazement, one of the men got out and proceeded to open a passage in the side of the mountain. "Did you see that?" Spencer hissed with excitement.

"They painted a wooden door to look like rock! It's brilliant!"

"Shhh," Winnie hushed. Turning to Spencer to lay a cautioning hand on his arm, she accidentally kicked a small rock over the edge. Winnie sat frozen in terror as the stone rolled down the slope, taking others with it. Then it smacked the back of the Odyssey, causing a thick, metallic clunk.

"Did you hear that?" the driver of the Odyssey asked.

"Hear what?" the other man said, standing by the entrance.

"Something rolled down and hit the car." The operator got out of his seat and began to scan the tops of the surrounding walls with a flashlight.

"Duck, Winnie," Spencer whispered, hastily pushing her head to the ground.

"Up there!" the man said, waving the flashlight in the direction of the kids. "I thought I saw somethin' movin'."

"Hey, Billy, it's prob'ly one of them Indian spirits that haunts the canyons!" The speaker put a quaver in his tone, trying to sound spooky.

"That ain't funny, Ray! You know I don't like them stories," Billy, the driver, yelled.

"There ain't nothin' out there, and there ain't

no such thing as an Indian spirit. Now get in and drive," Ray ordered.

Staring for a second, as if frightened to turn his back on the cliff, Billy hesitated before going back to the Odyssey.

The vehicle drove into the opening in the rock face and out of sight. Then Ray closed the door behind them, sealing the mountain once again.

Spence jumped up and pointed. "Did you see that? Just like in the Pied Piper story! There's a secret hideout in there."

"It's been way over half an hour," Winnie said in a worried voice. "Mike and Ben are in trouble. We better go get Smitty before something bad happens." Winnie and Spence hurried back to their quad runners and raced off toward Ambrosia.

Moving quietly through the tunnel, Mike used the beam of the flashlight to examine the interior. The inside was high ceilinged, and some of the rocks dripped slimy brown wetness.

Mike could tell that Ben was feeling nervous about the trip and could be claustrophobic. He was sweating, but he told himself it was only because of the heaviness of the atmosphere. The odor was disgusting and reminded Mike of a mildew-smelling silver mine he had visited in Virginia City, Nevada.

The floor of the cave was smooth and suspiciously free of loose rocks. Mike stopped to study the surface. "It's not natural," he observed.

"OK, Mike," Ben whined, "we've seen it. Now, let's go."

"Not yet. Notice how clean this floor is? It's like it's been swept."

"So? Maybe the spiders and snakes that live here are neatness freaks or something. Let's go!"

Mike pointed the flashlight into the blackness ahead. "There's a bend in the tunnel up there. Let's see what's around the corner."

"But out is this way . . . ," Ben protested.

Suddenly Mike shut off his light and pressed himself against the wall. "Shhh!" Mike warned in an urgent whisper. "I thought I saw another light!" He slowly moved his head around the rock and took a longer look. Then he saw what it was. An Odyssey off-road vehicle stood parked in the cave. Mike figured out that his light must have reflected off of a headlight.



"Mike," Ben said, "I don't think this is such a good idea. I mean—"

"Quiet," Mike hissed. "How do you expect to get to the bottom of this mystery if you chicken out now?" Advancing again, Mike inspected the

Odyssey and found a fluorescent lamp on the front that was tinted purple.

"Must be a black light," he said, "but I wonder what that would be for."

He then noticed a strange box hooked on to the back. When he looked closer, he saw that the box contained three rows of brushes that were attached to mechanical arms.

"That's how they're doing it," Mike said. "The brushes cover the tracks as they drive." The section of the cavern they were in appeared to be a storage area. There were pallets of stacked equipment covered with blue tarps. On one there were gas cans—at least thirty by Mike's guess.

Suddenly Mike heard a low rumble behind them. "C'mon," Mike urged. "We gotta get hidden." He shut off the light again and pulled Ben toward the parked ATV, and they climbed under it. Mike crawled forward to peek out from behind the front left tire. The rumble of the engine from the arriving vehicle grew as it rounded the bend in the cavern. A glowing green line appeared on the floor of the cavern as if by magic.

"Aliens!" Ben hissed. "Death ray!"

"Take it easy," Mike said. "It's only a black light—like glow in the dark."

The line zigzagged on the floor and then shot

up the wall where a fluorescent-pink sign said STOP.

A second Odyssey came to a halt, and the driver shut off the engine. Someone also turned off the black light, and the tunnel was dark again. Then two men in overalls with an electric lantern got out of the Odyssey and began unloading boxes.

"Now we're getting somewhere," Mike whispered. "What do you suppose that is? Drugs? Stolen stuff? They got it all planned out—a trail that you can only follow with black light and a way to cover their tracks behind them."

"Yeah . . . really cool," Ben murmured back, a frantic tone in his words. "Mike, wake up and smell the pizza! It doesn't matter what it is! Those guys won't be happy to see us! Let's get out of here!"

Mike began crawling to the far side of the ATV.

"Where are you going?" Ben pleaded. "Wait!"

"Quiet," Mike said. "Let's follow and see what's going on here."



"I'll wait for you here," Ben whispered.

Mike knew that once the tunnel got dark, Ben would come running. Sure enough, when the criminals rounded the corner, the storage cavern was pitch-black again, and he heard Ben come shuffling along after him.

"Uh, Mike . . . wait up!" Ben called.

A chugging engine noise could be heard in the next cavern ahead, and a faint light increased as the boys slipped behind some crates and under a tarp. They positioned themselves to see what was in the last section of the grotto.

Peering out through a crack in the tarp flap, Mike saw that the engine noise came from a generator that was powering the lighting. As Mike watched, the two men he had seen earlier stacked boxes, and he saw a third man seated at a desk in the corner talking into a radio transmitter.

Mike could not get a real good look at the man until he turned around to examine something that one of the workers brought him. Mike felt sick when he realized who the man was.

"The stranger at the diner!" Mike whispered excitedly, then remembered that Ben had not seen the man.

"What?" Ben asked. "What stranger?"

"Never mind," Mike replied. "Just watch."

The man at the radio was broadcasting the familiar nonsense that they had heard when Spencer tuned in the radio. *"Ekul . . . kaej . . . eekldobe . . . korb . . . lechar."*

Unwrapping a cloth-covered object, the man at the radio displayed something that sparkled in the artificial lights.

"Gold!" Ben said. "They're making gold!"

"You don't make gold," Mike said. "You dig it up. And it's more likely that they're stealing it."

"Very nice, Ray," the stranger said in a British accent.

The man was not wearing a suit coat, and Mike saw that the man wore a pistol in a holster that hung under his left arm.

Noticing that Ben was shifting around, Mike glanced over at him to see what he was doing. "Quit moving. You're making too much noise."

"But, Mike," Ben said as he stared above Mike's head, "there's a scorp—"

"I don't care! Do you want to get us killed?"

"B-but—"

"Shhh!" Mike said a final time and looked back to the activity in the cave. Ben tapped his shoulder, and when Mike turned around ready to scold him again, Ben just pointed up to the tarp above him. A scorpion hung from the canvas over his head.



"Don't panic," Mike said. "If I sit still, it won't hurt me." The whisper had only just left his mouth when Mike spotted movement above Ben's head and saw an even larger scorpion clinging there. At the instant Mike saw it, the creature dropped!

"Yo! Crimony! Big scorpion!" Ben yelled.

Ben jumped up beneath the tarp, shaking his head to fling the scorpion off. He then ran out from beneath the canvas in one direction as Mike burst out from the other. They were face-to-face with some startled and very angry criminals.

# 10

Mike and Ben both realized what would happen if they did not get away. They ran for the mouth of the cavern with Mike in the lead.

"Run, Mike! Run!" Ben yelled as he puffed and panted.

One of the radioman's henchmen appeared out of the shadows in front of Ben. "Where do you think you're going?" he said with a cruel smile on his face.

Ben did not even slow down when he saw the man. Instead, he accelerated, hitting the man's midsection with all of his weight behind his right shoulder, knocking the man onto his back. Ben continued sprinting down the tunnel.

Mike had gotten as far as the storage cavern when he heard a noise ahead and ducked behind the pallet of gas cans. He saw Ben run past just as he hid himself, and waved frantically, trying to signal. The two men in coveralls were fast on Ben's trail, and when he stumbled in the dim light, they grabbed him by both arms and hauled him back toward the radio room. Mike heard Ben kicking and screaming, and several sharp cracks and pointed exclamations as Ben's heels crunched against shinbones. The sound of footsteps close by made Mike push himself against the gas cans and shrink down into the shadows. The idea that he was certainly sharing the gloomy canvas with more scorpions scampered through his mind.



"Michael," the voice of the radio operator called from the darkness. Mike wondered how the man knew his name, but then remembered Ben yelling it out as they ran.

"Michael," the cultured British accent called out again. "This is Mister Von Paris. Why don't you come out? You're just making it more difficult for all of us. We don't want to hurt you. If you insist on staying hidden, we'll have to punish you severely when we find you. And we *will* find you."

Mike heard Ben whimpering as they dragged him back to the radio room. "Michael," the man repeated, this time louder, with exasperation. "Come out now, or I will be forced to hurt your friend! And I know that you don't want that, now, do you?" The voice echoed deeply in the cave and seemed to surround Mike in the darkness.

Feeling sick and bewildered, Mike wondered why he had not listened to Smitty and kept out of this mess. He heard the crunch of dirt as another step fell close to him. He slowly turned, then gasped to see the man peering straight at him, not quite able to make him out in the shadows. Maybe there was still time.

Mike grabbed the nearest gas can, and adrenaline surged through his body, making his head spin as he readied himself. "Ah, there you are," Von Paris said as his eyes finally adjusted to the light and he spotted Mike.

At that instant Mike seized the empty gas can and swung the metal container straight for the man's face. A dull thud and a hollow boom resulted, and the figure of the radio operator fell under the blow.

Mike bolted toward the opposite flap of canvas when a hand grasped him around the ankle with a viselike grip. Lashing out with his other foot, Mike kicked at the man's face and got free of his grip. Completely turned around in the confusing darkness, Mike did not realize that he was running back toward the radio room until the light of the inner chamber swelled around him. By then it was too late to retrace his steps, so Mike jumped on top of the pallet under which he and Ben had first hidden just a few minutes earlier.

Ray made a grab for his legs, but Mike leaped over him, heading directly for the generator. He was determined to rescue Ben, and a plan had formed in his mind.

The man holding Ben's arm lunged for Mike as the boy ran past, but Ben began kicking and swinging his fists with all of his might. Reaching the throbbing generator, Mike threw the handle of the shutdown switch and plunged everything into pitch blackness.



By the faint light given off by the dials of the battery-operated radio set, Mike could still make out Ben's location. He could hear Ben struggling and the curses of the man trying to restrain him.

Running at full speed into Ben's captor, Mike punched him in the stomach, and both boys were up and racing for the cave entrance once again.

Shouting came from all around them. "Lights!" Ray yelled. "Billy! Fire up that generator! Switch on the tunnel lights!"

As Mike and Ben ran through the storage area and into the exit passage again, pale fluorescent lights began coming on in sequence behind them, as if chasing them down the cavern.

They almost made it. The boys passed the hole into which Ben and Mike had fallen. It could only be a little bit farther. . . .

"You have made me very angry!" Von Paris said sharply. "Now, you will stop and do exactly as I say!" He was sitting on a boulder at the last bend of the cave, holding a bloody handkerchief to his nose with his left hand. His other fist held a gun. Ben gasped a ragged breath that was almost a sob. "I would appreciate it," Von Paris continued, his voice gradually rising, "if you would cooperate. I will not be as merciful as I have before *if you don't!*" Ben slumped to the floor of the tunnel in exhaustion. "Michael," the man said in a now quiet voice that was somehow even more menacing, "get your friend up and move!"



A tumbleweed blew past the dimly lit sheriff's office. From behind the hill in back of the building, engines growled, and the headlights of two quad runners searched the sky like beacons. Fishtailing, Winnie and Spencer skidded to a stop in front. A cloud of dust chased them as they threw off their helmets and ran to the door. They rushed into the office, dashing past Arlene.

"Hey, you kids can't just barge in like that!" Arlene screeched as they burst into Sheriff Smitty's private office.

Smitty sat at his desk holding a letter. On the back of the envelope, in bold red print, were stenciled the letters *FBI.* Scrambling to hide it, he crammed the letter into a drawer.

"What now?" Smitty asked in an exasperated tone.

Winnie, struggling to catch her breath, gasped. "The old mine tunnel . . . Mike and Ben went in—"

Spencer interrupted, "And then an Odyssey with two men—"

"Some kind of weird purple light, and that howling sound . . . ," Winnie panted.



"It was an ultraviolet beam that lit up—," Spencer said, cut off again by Winnie.

"Mike and Ben may be in trouble," she said anxiously. "They need help!"

Smitty stood up. "Hold it! Wait up! Mike and Ben are where?" Putting on his official voice of authority, he said, "Slow down and start from the beginning."

Moments later, the frosted-glass door flew open. Out charged Wynona and Spence followed by Smitty, buckling on his gun belt.

"Arlene! Get FBI-Phoenix . . . Special Agent Adams. Tell him Operation Whisper has broken wide open! Tell him Navajo Mesa, southeast corner, pronto," he instructed. "You kids go get in my truck," he told Winnie and Spence. As soon as they were gone, Smitty turned back to Arlene and remarked, "Tell Phoenix, 'Approach with caution; possible hostage situation.'" Then he grabbed his tan Stetson cowboy hat and sprinted for the door.

Mike and Ben sat tied to chairs that were placed back-to-back close to the radio set. Their hands were fastened behind them, and they bumped each other's arms. Von Paris had sent Billy and Ray out of the tunnel to look around for other "snoopers," as he called them. Mike prayed that Winnie and Spence had gotten enough warning to be far, far away and were even now bringing help!

The handkerchief stuffed in Mike's mouth as a gag made it hard to breathe. The handkerchief tasted of the radioman's blood, and it made Mike sick.

*"Manto inog . . . Ekul korb tellub . . . ,"* the man mumbled into the transmitter.

*New code,* Mike thought. *Wonder what he's saying? Probably that they have caught a couple of snooping kids and he needs to have them disposed of.* Mike slumped at this idea.

Some hard object was pressed against Mike's bruised leg by the hard wooden frame of the chair. Something in Mike's swirling thoughts urged him that this was important, that he should pay attention. He focused on the painful lump and suddenly remembered—it was the compass.

Mike leaned back and thumped the back of his head against Ben's to get his attention.

"Mmmmmm," Ben moaned, and Von Paris glared at them.

*No!* Mike thought urgently. *Be quiet!*

The radioman went back to work, and Mike leaned his head over to the right and bumped Ben's head with his own. This time Ben looked over his shoulder, and Mike nodded down to where the bulge of the compass stuck out of Mike's pants pocket.



Slow at first to grasp the meaning of the motion, Ben's eyes widened when the idea became clear. The compass case was full of shards of broken glass, fragments that could be used to cut them free! Ben fumbled with his hands and maneuvered them to reach for the compass.

*That's it,* Mike thought. *You have it.*

Ben's fingers bumbled with the brass case. It took him several tries to pull the compass free, stopping and trying to appear very still whenever Von Paris turned to look at them. He almost had it loose, then bobbled it. Mike and Ben held their breath as the compass balanced on the edge of Mike's pocket. A false move and it would clatter to the floor, giving away their plan!

Taking a deep breath, Ben wriggled his hands like tongs to grasp the instrument and pull it free. Working blind behind his back, he popped open the case and selected the biggest chunk of glass he could find and began sawing through the ropes.

It was a very long time before much progress was made, but Mike knew that the men had only used one rope, looping it around their wrists. If only one strand could be severed, they would be free!



Nearing the final cut, Ben slipped, nicking Mike's wrist. An involuntary gasp escaped Mike's throat at the sharp, slicing pain. In that instant, he was actually grateful for the gag that muffled his cry of pain. The radio operator rounded on them sharply but, seeing nothing out of place, turned back to his work.

In the next second, as Ben leaned hard on his improvised blade, the strands parted, and the boys' hands jumped apart. It was the greatest struggle yet to hold still and make it appear as though they were still bound.

Bracing himself for flight, Mike could feel the tenseness in Ben that indicated he was ready also. Almost by common thought, the boys recognized the moment when the time was right. Von Paris was absorbed in his broadcast, and the other two men were not around. With a sudden spring, Mike and Ben jumped up at the same instant. The chairs crashed over, and they again raced for freedom.

"Stop!" they heard the radioman yell after them.

Pulling out the bloody gag, Mike yelled, "We've got to make it this time!"

Von Paris started after them, leaping up from his stool and shouting. He had gone no more than six feet when the cord of the radio headphones still over his ears jerked him to a sudden stop, spinning him awkwardly around.



Mike rounded another corner in the mine's seemingly endless maze. Beads of sweat ran down his face. Ben panted, struggling to keep up. Would they make it to the tunnel's entrance? Mike's heart pounded, for there in the darkness, danger was only a few steps behind.

They reached the area where the Odysseys were parked. Mike glanced over his shoulder and saw Ben swerve toward the machines. Hanging from the ignition, as if an angel had placed them there, were the keys. "Mike, the Odyssey!" Ben puffed. "The keys are here!" Mike raced over to join Ben, and the two jumped in.

Ben turned the key and the engine revved. He threw the Odyssey into reverse just as Von Paris emerged from the dark tunnel behind them.

Von Paris grabbed Mike by his shirtsleeve, trying to drag him out of the bucket seat. The seam of the shirt ripped and split, while the criminal ran alongside shouting for them to stop. Ben swerved to the right, bashing the man into some crates and knocking loose his grip.

Around two more corners, a darker mass showed ahead of the boys, but there was no rush of air or gleam of light to show that they had reached the outside. "Ben!" Mike shouted. "The opening is blocked! We're trapped!"

"Hold on!" Ben yelled back.

Outside, the two henchmen returned from their unsuccessful search. Hearing the echoing roar of the engine down in the tunnel, the men looked at each other with surprise. Seconds later,

Mike and Ben plowed through the wooden wall that camouflaged the tunnel's entrance, just missing the men as they dove out of the way. The thin wood panels splintered into a thousand pieces as the Odyssey burst out into the desert.

Moments later, Von Paris drove up in the other ATV. He was sputtering with anger. "Get in, you idiots! We have to catch them!"

Ben drove blindly through the moonless desert. The spinning tires sent rocks and dirt sailing behind. "I can't see anything. Can you find the light switch?" he urged, narrowly missing a boulder.

Mike hastily felt around on the panel between the seats. "Here it is," he said, flipping a toggle. The black light mounted on the front of the frame lit up, illuminating the rocks and tumbleweeds with a purple fluorescent glow.

The ultraviolet light revealed a shimmering green hieroglyphic figure painted on a boulder in their path. The brakes screeched as Ben stomped on the pedal and cranked the wheel hard to the left. The Odyssey lurched up on two wheels, barely avoiding disaster! Another swerve and the ATV bounced back down hard, racing off in the direction indicated by the outstretched right arm of the skeletal figure.

"Can't you go any faster?" Mike yelled. "They're right behind us!"

"It's floored," Ben answered. The engine sputtered, coughing out a thick cloud of smoke. The vehicle in hot pursuit of the boys slowed, its own blacklight projector barely penetrating the thick fog of dust and exhaust from the Odyssey ahead.

"I see the next marker," Mike shouted to Ben. "It's over to the right." Ben swung the speeding vehicle in a wide turn in the direction of the next figure.

Through a cloud of billowing dust, Von Paris saw them turn. "I'll get them," he said, cutting across the wide arc and narrowing the gap.

"They're catching up, Ben!" shouted Mike with a frightened glance over his shoulder. Ben pushed down harder on the accelerator, not noticing how fast they were approaching a deep ravine.

"Ha!" Von Paris laughed. "They are headed for the canyon! We'll catch them there!" The pursuing Odyssey roared alongside the arroyo, skidding to a stop broadside to the ravine.



Mike turned to see where their enemies had gone. "They stopped," he said excitedly. "I wonder why?" Then with a terrified realization, he shouted, "Ben, look out!"

Ben, eyes wide and mouth open, yelled, "Ahhhhh . . ." It was too late. The Odyssey flew wildly through the air as if trying to leap the canyon in an attempt to escape. Mike braced himself, ducking his head.

The front of the ATV crashed into the slope on the far side of the ravine, the blacklight projector splintering in an eruption of flame. The Odyssey flipped over several times, bouncing like a toy truck dropped down a flight of steps. The metal frame struck showers of sparks, while sliding upside down. It skidded on its roof down the shale rock, finally coming to a rest at the bottom of the canyon.

## 11

Retrieve them," Mike heard Von Paris say. "Or what's left of them."

From where he had crawled to conceal himself in the brush, Mike watched the dark, hulking shadows of the two workmen walk toward the overturned Odyssey. His upper lip felt funny—numb and swollen. A thin trickle of blood ran down to his chin. Mike was afraid to move even enough to wipe it off.

"They're not here!" one of the men yelled.

"Blast!" Von Paris exploded. "They can't be far. We would have seen them running. You and Ray start looking. I'll watch from up here."

The men trampled the tangle of wiry bushes where Mike and Ben lay shivering. Both boys were lying with their stomachs pressed to the ground, hugging the bases of the thickest tumbleweeds they could find.

Searching close to where the boys crouched, the man named Billy smashed the bushes with a shovel. He swung it from side to side, chopping the brittle weeds into fragments and crunching the tool into boulders. Mike smelled the pungent odor from the shattered plants. It sickened him to imagine that the next impact of the blade could be his head.

The shovel splintered another clump of sage, and a piece of dry branch flew through the air, hitting Ben in the side of the face. Mike heard his stifled yelp, but the noise of the crunching underbrush covered the sound. At last the man turned away and continued on to another thicket farther off.



Mike's breath sounded so loud to him that he was afraid that the searchers would hear it. When he tried to hold it to slow it down, his heartbeat pounded in his ears. Then when he had to gasp for breath again, it seemed to Mike that he had made more noise than a truck engine in the stillness.

A flashlight beam swung around, hitting the brush just over Mike's head. The circle of illumination made the shadows of the branches flicker and crawl as if thousands of black snakes were slithering through the brush. When the light passed close to him again, it took all Mike's willpower to stay still.

*I've got to control my fear,* Mike thought. *God help me stay cool.* He noticed that Ben was not doing too good either. He was breathing hard and looking around at every shadow as if it were a snake or another scorpion.

Ray, the other criminal bossed by Von Paris, stepped close, the dirt crunching under his hiking boots just on the other side of the brush from Mike. A shovel swung wildly and crashed down between Mike and Ben. They both stared at the shiny blade gleaming in the reflected light of the flash. It occurred to Mike that it was brand-new and that it might dig into his skull before it was ever used for dirt. But then the man went away again.

The workmen seemed to vanish, and Von Paris walked forward into the brush and spoke. "Boys," he said in a deliberately kind, coaxing tone.

"Why don't you come out? I know you must be hurting after that bad crash. We can . . . help."

Mike thought he heard stifled laughter from behind him in the darkness. He figured that Von Paris must have sent his henchmen out to sneak up on them.

A moving shape right beside Mike's elbow startled him, making him jump. A jackrabbit appeared under another clump of sage. Mike wished that it would go away, fearing that the crooks might come to investigate the noise it made and stumble across the hiding place. The rabbit, frightened by the crunch of weeds under booted feet, leapt up and over a four-foot-high tumbleweed. "There!" shouted Von Paris, pivoting toward the flashing shape. The roar of a pistol erupted as the criminal turned and fired. He shot twice more as the jackrabbit bounded away.

A chorus of angry yells came from the two accomplices. "Hey!" Ray shouted. "You trying to kill us too? Take it easy with that thing!" The men came in from the surrounding darkness and joined their boss next to the overturned Odyssey.



"So much for the sweet talk, huh?" Mike heard Billy say. "They know you'll shoot them now. I'd stay hidden too."

"Quiet, you fool!" Von Paris hissed. "Do you want them to hear?"

But Mike and Ben had already heard and knew that Billy was right. They could not come out or they would end up worse off than the rabbit.

The voices retreated, and Mike could not hear them for a long time. He thought it might be safe to move a little to get a better look at where they had gone.

After only the slightest movement, a bright light shone right in his face, stabbing his eyes like a knife blade. Von Paris was perched on top of the overturned Odyssey, aiming the spotlight with one hand and his gun with the other. "Got you!" he said. "Stand up and come out." No sugary words now. The voice of Von Paris dripped evil like snake venom.

Mike and Ben obeyed. A slight breeze picked up, and Mike felt the desert wind for what he thought would be his last time. Von Paris kept the spotlight directly in their faces as they moved toward the vehicle.



The bright shaft from the spotlight wavered and flickered. Mike saw Von Paris shake it with impatience, as if the batteries were failing. Glancing at Ben, Mike was startled to see an odd grin on his friend's face. Mike thought that Ben had completely lost his mind; fear must have driven him crazy: He was smiling.

The spotlight dimmed and then flared again.

Ben heard a now familiar low howling, and suddenly he understood.

The spotlight died completely, and a green glow appeared from behind the hill down which the Odyssey had tumbled. Then the large blue-white light appeared. It slid across the sky as he'd seen it do before, and while the crooks were distracted, Mike and Ben dove for the bushes again.

The howling was very loud now, and the beam of light circled above Von Paris and his men. It stabbed the leader, pinning his silhouette against the dark hill like a bug impaled on a pin. Von Paris stepped backward on the Odyssey's frame and fell with a crash, then tried to scramble away on his back.

"I bet little green men come out and eat the bad guys," Ben laughed.

Then Mike heard an amplified voice from out of the light beam: "Put up your hands! This is the FBI! Put up your hands!" Reluctantly, their faces contorted into masks of rage, the three men complied.



Truck headlights came out of the darkness as Smitty's patrol vehicle rolled up, and Winnie, Spence, and Smitty all got out.

Mike smiled at Ben. "Little green men, huh?"

Smitty walked toward the men with his pistol drawn and made them spread-eagle against the ATV. He pulled out their weapons and threw them on the ground, then handcuffed three sets of wrists. Winnie and Spence ran to Mike and Ben, and as they watched, the mysterious light touched down in a whirling cloud of dust.

The Last Chance Detectives stood in the cavern talking about what had happened. Smitty spoke to Ben. "Do you understand now why I couldn't back you up on what we saw out there? That supersecret whisper helicopter was searching for the crook's hideout. It has the electronic gear to shut down engines, which is what happened to the quad and my truck."

"So you didn't think we could keep our mouths shut," Ben retorted. "Is that it?"

Ben saw the other three kids staring at him with very pointed expressions. One of Winnie's eyebrows was raised almost to the top of her head, and even Mike had a lopsided grin. He suddenly realized that they also thought he would have blabbed, and he had to admit they were probably right. "OK, OK!" he agreed. "I give!"

"Besides," Smitty continued, "the gang was watching things in town. You kids would have been in *more* danger if they knew you were onto them."

Mike thought about that for a moment. "Yeah," he said, remembering. "Von Paris was at the diner the night Ben was lost!"

"That's right," Smitty said. "And it's a good thing for Ben that guy didn't find him."

Ben shuddered. "So what exactly did they do?"

"Von Paris is wanted in six countries for art and jewel theft, among other things. Capturing this gang solves more than just the museum robbery."

The group stood in silence until Ben broke out with, "That's it then, another case successfully solved by the Last Chance Detectives! Oh boy, just wait till the newspapers get wind of this! We'll be famous! Six o'clock news . . . magazine interviews . . . a miniseries."

Smitty crossed his arms and stared at Ben. "Sorry to let you down, Ben," he said, "but I'm afraid not. The whole operation and especially the helicopter have to forever remain a secret. The FBI still hopes to round up the crooked collectors and some other accomplices, so all this is classified top secret."



Ben looked disappointed, but Mike nudged him, grinned, and raised an eyebrow. Ben nodded, and the four friends gave a loud Last Chance salute! Then as the four stood with right hands raised, Mike held his other hand over the compass and the Bible in his pocket. Sheriff Smitty swore the Last Chance Detectives to secrecy in the case of the *Mystery Lights of Navajo Mesa.*